KING CONSORT

GOTHA AETURNUM

J.R. GRAY

Published by J.R. Gray
© 2018. J.R. Gray
King Consort
All Rights Reserved.

ISBN: 9781982900533

Cover Image: Deposit Photo
Cover Design: Rebel Graphics
Formatting: Rebel Graphics

To my grandmother who loved me no matter what.

LOUIS

Faking heterosexuality 101, don't go out drinking all night and then show up severely hung over to tea with the Queen. Exactly where I happened to be on a Saturday morning. Maybe I was still drunk, I'm not even sure at this point. All I remember was Anne kept filling my gin and tonic, and I lost count.

"You look ghastly," the Queen commented as I started to pour myself some tea with shaky hands. Then she looked at her watch and tsked.

"I didn't except to be summoned so early in the morning."

"It's two in the afternoon."

"So early in the morning." I met her gaze, and she gave me a flat look.

"I ought to disinherit you. You and that disgrace of a French name."

"You don't have any better options, and you shouldn't have let father marry French royalty if you didn't want the heritage tainted."

She muttered under her breath. Something my grandmother loved to do when dealing with people who annoyed her. Like the Prime Minster. He was forever asking her "What?" and she'd smile and say, 'You really do need to have your hearing checked, Mr. Gladstone. I didn't say a thing.'

One of the oldest tricks in her book. And she had many considering she was the longest ruling sovereign in British history. Frankly, she needed to start writing them down so I could have a few of them.

"I just can't die." She scoffed into her tea.

"You know, if you acted like this for the public, they'd probably like you better."

"I don't need to be liked. They respect me."

I brought the steaming cup of tea to my lips and moaned at the first taste. It wasn't that the tea was particularly good, but more that my body was in desperate need of fluid after last night's events.

"I'm sure they'll respect me when the time comes."

"Not the way the rumors are going."

"Rumors." I flashed her a wry smile. "No proof, just whispers." And since the rumors were quite purposefully cultivated, I wanted them to remain, but I wasn't going to tell her that. It was all about slight of hand.

She looked at the ceiling. Like she was having a conversation with her dead husband. Something she did often. "The country needs stability. Especially after…" She gave me a look as she trailed off. She didn't want to say it, but I knew what she meant. After the disappointment my sister was.

Neither of us liked to say it out loud because we both knew it wasn't her fault. But the papers and public opinion had crucified her long ago. It was hard enough to be a teen without your every action and mistake used for public consumption.

"What does my being a whore have to do with stability? This is expected from…" I made air quotes. "The most eligible bachelor in Britain."

"I should have never suggested you could marry a commoner."

"What then? Arrange a marriage for me with some other royal and taint the bloodline further?"

"We haven't had issues with that in at least a century."

"Only because it was exactly one hundred years ago your grandfather made his favorite horse a knight and then appointed him to the House of Commons!" I got a little worked up about family history. I forced myself to calm down as my head started to pound. "A horse being a knight. I can't even process." If it wasn't embarrassing, it would be funny.

"Which is why the country needs stability."

"I wasn't trying to make your point." I poured more sugar in my tea. Almost half the little china cupful. It had a name, something I'd learned in etiquette classes, but I couldn't remember with this headache.

"What are you trying to do then, Louis, give yourself diabetes?" she said, nodding to the sugar.

I glared as I set down the sugar bowl. "I need to replace my electrolytes."

"And we've come back full circle." She put her cup on her saucer, which she held in her other hand. She was the image of eloquent and distinguished from an era mostly forgotten as she was something like eighty-seven. Although she barely seemed over sixty. "I'm sending you on tour. With Anne. I—" She pursed her lips, choosing her words. "I can't be bothered to go, and it's long overdue. It's your duty."

"It's my duty, I'll give you that, but didn't I do enough in the military stationed all over the planet?"

"You retired two years ago, and what have you done since then?"

Honestly, nothing, but I wasn't going to tell her that. Now if only the brain cells I had left would put together a coherent excuse.

"I thought so."

"I've done a lot of work at home." I was still drawing blanks. It was like the gin had wiped my mind clean.

"You've done a minimal amount."

"Working five days a week is a minimal amount?"

"It's possible."

I didn't try and argue any more. She had her own idea of what was acceptable.

"Where am I going? Please tell me Africa." I was dying to get back there. I'd spent a good amount of time there in my early twenties, and honestly I didn't know why I hadn't gone back yet.

"No."

"Australia?"

"No."

My eyes narrowed, and I looked at her hard. "Somewhere in the Caribbean where I can work on my tan? Then I'll come back all fit and brown. Would be great for the papers." I was more hopeful than hoping she'd actually do it. There were a lot of countries in the commonwealth she ruled over, but not many which would require an entire tour.

"Sorry, no." She wasn't sorry.

That only left one place.

"Not Cananda."

A smile turned up the corners of her tiny pink lips. Almost like she was taunting me. "Yes, Canada."

"In the bloody winter?" London was dreary, but we were mostly spared terrible winters. "Is this a punishment?"

"It's not a punishment."

"Are you banishing me? This is a banishment, isn't it?"

"No."

I set down my tea and sat back. "Then what is it?"

"I think it will be good for you to get out of the country. Meet new people. Anne could use some good press. It's been two years, and some positive press coverage will do her good."

"Meet new people?" There was more behind her words than she was telling me.

"Yes." And the smile was back. Lord, I could only imagine what she was like in the prime of her rule. Ruthless. I bet it was a sight to be seen.

"This is about me finding a wife, isn't it?" I was horrified. For more than one reason.

"The biggest whore in Britain shouldn't have an issue finding someone he can stand to have at his side. I'm not asking you to propose as soon as you're introduced."

I blank stared. "I could meet someone here."

"I'm quite sure you've been through all the eligible women in the country."

She was so wrong, but I wasn't about to ruin my perfectly

crafted and cultivated rumors.

"You think the best way to get me to find someone to settle down with is to send me to Canada? You think the future of the crown is a Canadian?"

"I think a little diversity in our blood would serve us well. You did state that we are too inbred."

And now she was using my own words against me. "But Canada? In the winter?"

"Take a coat."

"Couldn't we go to some place warm...like Australia?"

"You object to Canada, but our former prison colony is acceptable?"

"The—" I have to cough to cover what almost came out of my mouth. "Women are hotter there?" I said it too much like a question, and she narrowed her eyes shrewdly. "I'm not looking for a bride." It was a bad cover.

"Then Canada shouldn't matter. And I'll send you wherever I please. It will be good for your sister."

"Do you think she can handle it?"

"I think getting her away from her normal group is preferable, and it's been two years."

"You think she's going to relapse? Because nothing about being in a different country will stop her. Remember Vegas?"

"I'm trying to get her out of the constant negative news cycle and into something positive, Louis."

"So I'm the babysitter?"

"You'll have the regular team of people."

"Do you think me being there will stop her from going out every night?"

She tittered her little laugh. "Hardly, as your current state would indicate."

"I don't go out like she does."

"And for that I am grateful. I'm sure there will be enough sport there to keep you entertained. You have to be bored of the population here."

"Women turn eighteen every day." And by women I meant men. I did love the little goth things. The more black eyeliner the better. They had such a hatred and loved to take it out on me in bed. I didn't indulge often. I'd hardly fucked as many as she imagined, but when I did... I nearly groaned out loud just thinking of the last time. It had been six months at least since I'd had any fun at all. Between keeping up my image and the worry the truth would get back to my grandmother, I was careful.

She pulled a face. "Please, please, for the love of your country, check IDs."

"Doug does that for me when he has them sign NDAs."

She was back to pinching the bridge of her nose. "Maybe with all the layers everyone will be wearing in Canada you'll have enough time to get to know their name before their clothes come off, and you can form some type of relationships."

It killed me to let her keep believing I was this gigantic douche, but what could I do? Seem as celibate as I was? It was hard enough to keep the rumour mill at bay.

"I'll do my best."

There wasn't anyone in the world who didn't know my face, so my chances of finding someone to hook up with in Canada were no better. I would just play babysitter to Anne and get to know my hand better than I already did. What I really needed was another trip to a Russian sex party. I pressed my eyes closed. All the anonymous sex to be had, and no one cared who I was in the communist hell hole.

"It's settled then. We'll talk details after the state dinner tomorrow."

I groaned. I really didn't want to have dinner with the American president. "Can I leave tonight?"

"Now this is the enthusiasm I wanted, but no."

LOUIS

"What in the fresh hell is this?"

My sister looked over at me as she pulled her hood over her head. "Winter."

"If by winter you mean hell." I braced and tried to keep my lazy smile on my face when all I wanted to do was grimace and run back into the jet we'd just stepped off. I had an appearance to keep up, even if Anne didn't give a rat's arse about her title.

"It's called a coat."

"I have an overcoat on."

She surveyed what I was wearing before turning back to the slew of cameras and giving them a princess wave. I wasn't even sure where she'd learned how to do that.

"It might suffice in London this time of year, but you need a parka here." She poked what I could only describe as a marshmallow contraption.

I slid my glove free hands into my pockets. "I don't want to look like a—" I rethought my words before I uttered them. "Michelin Man."

"Warm, you mean you don't want to appear warm?" She looked at me over the tops of her sunglasses. "You're such a dandy."

It was bright as fuck here, but I didn't want the glasses interfering with my image. Men just couldn't pull them off when dressed up as well as women. So here I was squinting with my balls frozen to my leg. Boxers were a must tomorrow, even though I'd sworn them off ages ago.

I stuck out my chin, giving her the smallest amount of attitude. "Isn't that the literal definition of my job? Think about it for a moment."

She pulled the zip cord on her hood. "Good thing I'm not the heir."

A normal prince would love to go on tour. It's out of the direct eye of the crown, and in theory away from those people who gave a shit about what the royal blood did. In reality, the entire world cared. The paparazzi followed us everywhere, and we were on just as many magazines in the U.S. as the UK. I didn't dare to hope to find Canada any different.

"Why does Canada have to be this cold?"

"We aren't even in Canada anymore, you twat."

I looked at her like she was stupid, or worse, high. "Where do you think we are, Anne?"

"Chicago."

"You could have told me. Why are we even here?" I looked around trying to see the difference between Toronto and Chicago. I couldn't tell, nor did I care. The entire city was coated in a grimy layer of salt and leftover snow. Thick rolling clouds created an atmosphere of depression I wasn't ready to deal with. Grey skies, grey buildings, grey tinted streets.

"I added a pit stop, since duty doesn't start for two days." She grinned over at me.

"Our visas aren't for the U.S." I was starting to panic we were going to cause a diplomatic incident.

"I had Doug do it for me. Will you calm down. I'm not an idiot anymore, and I'd appreciate if you stopped treating me like one."

I couldn't help it. I'd spent too many years protecting her, and whether she needed it or not, it was my default position. "I apologise."

"Thank you. Now, will you relax?"

I slipped into our standard Range Rovers, and she rolled her eyes as she climbed in beside me.

"What now?" I asked.

She gestured at my posture. "This isn't a state dinner."

"I have a hard time turning it off. Too much training."

"I'm so glad I didn't turn out like you." She bumped our shoulders together. "I have a surprise for you."

I cringed.

"Have a little faith."

"I can't help it."

She looked exasperated. "It's a wonder I try and do anything nice."

I had a flashback to the last time she tried to 'help me out' and shuddered.

"It wasn't that bad," she said, as if she could read my mind.

"I'm pretty sure there is still a photo of me holding that magazine."

"They are everywhere. Just google yourself. It's the first thing that comes up, but I'm sure you put it to good use." She made a jack off motion and wiggled her brows.

I had used the magazine frequently, before porn was so readily available on the internet, but she wasn't aware in the slightest it wasn't the women I was interested in. Thankfully now it was as easy as a scroll through Tumblr to keep me satisfied.

"You should say thanks now."

"Not a chance. This could still be a disaster."

"Isn't it the thought that counts?"

"I would say yes, but no, not after last time." I let my head fall back to the headrest. There was too much on my mind to worry about why Anne had suddenly needed to go to Chicago, but I was curious. "So why Chicago? Yes, I noticed you avoided answering."

She chewed her lip a little, and I just hoped it wasn't drugs. "I'm meeting a friend, okay?"

I left it at that, because it wasn't worth knowing more. Plausible deniability.

We weren't at the hotel long before Anne was in my room throwing clothes at me. She rifled through my garment bags until she found a shirt to her standards, making quite a few quips about my boring and formal taste.

"Don't you have anything with polka dots or a pattern? You do realise what year it is, don't you? These are all so plain."

"Do I look like a hipster to you?"

"With our genes, your beard would come in red. Don't do that."

"I'm blond." I looked in the mirror, buttoning up the shirt she'd handed me. I didn't think my facial hair would come in red. Well at least not all of it. "It would probably be tri-coloured, if we're honest."

"I bet the Prime Minster would love that. I change my vote. Grow it out when you become King and then look him dead in the eyes and see if he can keep a straight face."

I looked at her in the mirror as I tied my tie. "Grandmother will be Queen for another fifty years. I'm sure we'll be three Prime Ministers on by that point."

She lifted one bony shoulder. "Maybe you'll never have to be King."

I wasn't sure if it was the remnants of the drug addiction or the pressure to stay a size six, but she was much too thin. It worried me. But she swore she was doing so much better. How could I question it and not look like an arsehole?

"What a stroke of luck that would be." I regretted it as soon as the words were out of my mouth. Her eyes were dead as I tried to look at her again. All the joy had fled. Our father had gotten out of being King by going to an early grave, and I didn't think Anne would ever get over it. Who could blame her really? It was hard enough to be a public figure without also being in mourning.

The shadows were gone from her face as quickly as they'd appeared. She was all smiles as she strung a necklace around her neck. "Louis?" she asked, holding it out for me to clasp.

I stepped up behind her and fixed it in place.

"Louis?"

"What? I'm getting it."

"No," she said pointing at the television Doug had flipped on. FMZ was on the air. The American version of the gossip rags but televised.

I read the headline and blanched. "Fuck."

LOUIS

I instantly felt better when we were safely inside the VIP area of the club my sister had chosen. It was a seizure inducing kind of place, with bright flashing lights, music I could only describe as robotic, more beeps than actual instruments, and both men and women dancing in cages. Perfect place for the future King.

It wasn't that I had so much of an issue among the commoners, but this was a special kind of hell. I was swamped with women at every turn. The news had proclaimed a source close to the Queen said I was on the hunt for a wife. It was a tangle of highlights and high heels. Long limbs and bronzer. It was impossible to escape, but unless any of them were hiding a dick under their dress, they were going to be sorely disappointed.

When I found out who'd leaked my agreement with my grandmother, I was going to have them quartered.

"Thinking about killing people again?"

"How can you tell?"

"It's either that or you're eye fucking someone. I can't tell."

"If it were eye fucking, we'd already be in the bathroom." I had an appearance to keep up. "They are plenty eager."

"Nothing tickles your fancy?" She cocked her head. "Are you covering for something?"

"Ignore me. Too much stress." I was not here to start a bunch of rumours which would end in my removing myself from the line of succession. I needed to keep my gaze to myself.

"Just come on over and meet Elle." Anne grabbed my hand and pulled me towards her friend.

"No, not a chance."

"And why not?"

"Because I will not be introducing myself to anyone, and if your idea of a 'surprise' is to set me up with a sure thing, then no."

"Last week you were going on about Australians. What is your deal?"

"There are a lot of lines the monarchy will cross, but I can't do this one or that one."

"What are you talking about?"

"It's our former prison colony."

She looked at the ceiling and sighed. "How long ago was that?"

"At least two hundred years, but how would it look?"

"She's American."

"Which isn't any better. Look at who they elected." I waved her off, trying to come off as superior, which always annoyed her.

"You're such an elitist bastard." She lowered her voice. "And here they don't have this royalty nonsense. Americans don't understand it. I'm not asking you to marry anyone. I'm telling you to enjoy the anonymous sex party."

"I'm sorry?" I leaned in, sure I'd heard her wrong.

"Oops." Her eyes glinted.

"We can't."

"You don't want to, fine, but I'm going, and you can't stop me, so it's go with me and keep an eye on me like you promised, or go back to the hotel and pace."

I narrowed my dark eyes. "Anne, this trip is about cleaning up your image."

"It's a good thing my friend Ben has it covered."

"There is no way he can control it."

She got to her feet and looked around. "There is, and he does." She reached for my hand.

Reluctantly I took it. "Do we really have to do this?"

"Your security is distracted, and I have a car waiting outside the back door."

"We have to talk to Doug. He's going to kill me," I said in protest as she started to lead me towards the door. I knew I should stop, but I couldn't bring myself to.

"It's safe in there. All off duty cops working."

"At a sex club?"

"Ben is a pretty unique guy." We were out the door and back in the cold, but not for long. Like Anne had promised, there was a black SUV waiting. The friend she wanted me to meet was already there, and I growled at her as I slid into the backseat. She shoved in next to me, pushing me closer to Elle.

"Elle this is Louis, Louis this is Elle. Be nice. I like her."

"And where do you know Elle from?"

Elle looked me over with one brow raised. "This is the heir? The one no one can tame?"

I scoffed.

Anne nodded like this had been a long topic of conversation between them. "More like no one can put up with."

I elbowed her in the ribs. "Please, I have more than enough money to pay someone to put up with me."

"I see what you mean," Elle commented.

I was thankful it wasn't a long drive, as they spent most of it talking over me. There was even less of a chance I was going to marry Elle just because she and my sister were thick as thieves, and it would be my utter nightmare for her to have an accomplice.

We pulled up in front of a nondescript factory, in a long dead district, mostly filled with offices, I assumed. There wasn't a car for miles.

"I do believe you've been played."

Anne giggled. "You're so naive."

The SUV pulled up to a loading bay, the kind large trucks are unloaded into. There was a ramp, and when we pulled up, our driver dialed in a number, and the door started to rise.

"You're bringing me here to murder me, aren't you?"

"If I wanted to get rid of you, I wouldn't spend so much time getting my own hands dirty."

"How much have you thought about this?"

"Not a whole lot, but I could easily plant drugs on you."

I was a little terrified.

She smiled all sweet. "Don't cross me."

"Maybe I'm going to have you murdered after I take the crown."

"As if. You like me too much, and your penis is going to like me even more after your birthday present."

"I'm far from convinced."

As soon as we walked in the door, I was convinced. This was like no place I'd ever been to or heard of. There were writhing naked bodies on every surface.

"Told you."

LOUIS

Two weeks ago

His Royal Highness Louis Edward Albert Frederick of the House of Gotha, Prince of Wales, KG, KT, GCB, OM, AK, QSO, PC, ADC, Earl of Chester, Duke of Cornwall, Duke of Rothesay, Earl of Carrick, Baron of Renfrew, Lord of the Isles, and Prince and Great Stewart of Scotland, and I wanted to beat myself to death with the paper it was written on. It was so damn pretentious. I needed a drink to deal with this state stuff.

The President no one liked, offered his hand. I groaned in my head as I took it, and it was indeed like every video I'd seen of the man. He tried to 'win' the handshake by pulling my hand towards him. He even got this funny look on his orange face. It was sadly easy to beat. He tightened his bicep and narrowed his eyes. I kept my face neutral and tightened my grip. The man melted but refused to let go. It went on entirely longer than it ruddy should have, with plenty of awkward photos.

The queen cleared her throat, and I was beyond grateful when the great baboon let go. He hadn't even read the protocol sheet. The bloody bastard called me The Royal Highness and practically ignored my grandmother the actual Queen. I stood for pictures and smiled through the mind-numbing chatter at the state dinner. Usually they weren't this bad, but this one was particularly painful. I was going to have to talk to my grandmother about getting out of the next one. If this president was going to return during his remaining time in office, I was going to be sick or dead.

"If you think I didn't notice you were bored, I did," my grandmother whispered to me as we walked out of the state dining room.

"The whole room knew," I remarked. My grandmother was a terrifying queen, but she and I had an understanding. She let me run wild so to speak, as long as I didn't embarrass the crown and I kept myself out of the tabloids.

"And how do you think we look when you're looking at the ceiling half the time the President was speaking?"

"You know quite well you sat him next to me so you didn't have to hear him drone on."

"With the title comes control of the seating arrangements." She gave me the tight little smile she loved to give reporters when they weren't going to get an inch out of her.

"Ruthless tyrant."

"Someone has to be."

"If you could sit me next to an assistant next time. Or hell, I'd take one of his dull children over listening to that buffoon."

She laughed much the way she smiled. It was short, sweet,

and to the point. "I rather enjoyed watching it."

"You're so fucking evil."

"Language."

"You need to get over it. The times are changing."

"The title deserves the respect. I'm hoping you learn before I keel over."

"We all know you stole the bloody fountain of youth from Hitler when Churchill overran the Nazis."

"Stop telling people that. Parliament is startling to believe it."

"Those gasbags would believe anything at this point, but I know for a fact they don't."

"Enlighten me."

"Because I told them all you died when I was seven, and the royal household has an elaborate ruse to keep you 'ruling' the country until I'm of age."

She looked astounded.

"The Prime Minister went into a coughing fit when I told him your corpse was filled with animatronic worms, brilliant technology from MI6."

She pinched the bridge of her nose. "I don't know which is worse, that you probably did actually tell them that piece of rubbish or that they also probably believe it."

"I know Digsby believed it. He kept trying to work out how we got you to talk during your meetings."

She gave me the same look I wore meeting the president. "He didn't."

"I told him it was the most elaborate *Weekend at Bernie's* ever done."

"You undermine the crown."

"Every day I'm alive, but you're stuck with me."

"Your sister could rule."

We both laughed without humour. If I thought she could survive it, I'd let her.

"Sure, let me just disqualify myself and see how that goes for you."

She raised a brow at me, probably questioning how I would do such a thing, and it was probably a terrible idea for me to have said it, but at least she didn't ask about it.

"At least she's sober."

"At the moment."

We both loved Anne, but she'd been in and out of rehab since she could get her hands on coke, which probably had a lot to do with our father dying in front of her, but it was what it was.

"I'd actually feel a lot better about dying eventually if there were better heirs."

"Wait, you have been draining the youth of the country in order to stay alive, haven't you?"

"I'm a vampire. Best kept secret in the kingdom."

"No wonder you're so pale." I gave her a serious look. "I told you I'm not getting married a day before I'm thirty, and you agreed. I get to have my fun."

"And if I die?"

I gave her a flat look. "You're going to outlive me. So all you need is one of my children to take over in forty or fifty years."

"I'm ninety."

"And?"

She scoffed at me, like only an old English woman can.

"Thirty. Let me have until then, and I'll pop out all the damn heirs you want."

"You have less than two years. Don't you think it's time you choose the young lady? You do need time to court her."

I groaned. I hated every single time this came up. It made me feel like a liar, which I was, but I didn't want to think about it. "It doesn't matter, does it?"

"Of course it matters." She looked a little horrified, having loved her husband dearly while he was alive, but that wasn't in the cards for me.

I lifted one shoulder. "Okay. It matters. I'll be sure to get right on it."

I was sure I was breaking her heart. She hated to see me as a ladies' man, but since my dearly departed father was the same, she probably assumed it ran in our bloodline. What king didn't have dozens of mistresses? It was an easy facade to slip into.

"Redheads," she muttered.

"Strawberry blond," I countered. "I only have red highlights."

"Potato, tomato."

"From what I hear, it's your line the red comes from."

"I didn't say I was any better, but I did learn my place."

"No, you just had to become queen at twenty."

"So be happy you had this much time to live, but you have a duty to uphold, and there is nothing more important." She paused before going on. "When you return, you need to pick someone."

"I know," I said, and I was willing to throw out my happiness for her. I was passionate about the work we were doing, but to me, not letting my grandmother down was top of the list, and since Anne couldn't do it for me, I had to be the one. We were out of blood.

LOUIS

The present

It was a sight to take in. No one was concerned with who I was. Half the crowd was dancing with little more than scraps of fabric on, and the other half were tucked into not so dark corners in the midst of orgies and that was just what I could see from the large viewing window we walked past. I needed condoms.

There was a formal business type desk just past where we left our coats and checked our phones. We signed NDAs, which was new for me, but I was informed I wasn't even close to the most famous person who entered the premises. Everything went into a large steal box and was locked away. The key was given back to us, along with a wristband, which we were told would pay for everything on site and be charged to the account my sister had set up before coming.

This was quite the elaborate birthday gift. It was a shame I couldn't actually use it. I wasn't about to risk my sister finding out I preferred dick, even if I could find a place to escape to where she might not see me. I would have to live vicariously through all the people getting what they wanted and needed.

The doors we were directed to deposited us into the middle of the throng of people. Sweaty bodies everywhere, and less clothing than had been visible through the window.

My sister smiled at me. "Come on. I have to go see Ben, and I think there will be more to your liking upstairs."

"Up?" As I said it, I looked above us to find more levels and balconies, and then at the very top of the building there was a catwalk where a few people leaned over watching.

We rode a lift to the top where Anne showed her wristband. "You can get onto any level," she told me as we were waved through. "Up here is more casual, and there is a great bar."

What she hadn't said was most of the men and women were fully naked as well. My cock took notice and begged to be set free. I ignored the inclination, listening as she went on.

"A floor down is mostly for sale. You can rent just about anything to your taste, and take them anywhere in the building, but you know it's kind of like the shop."

"Excuse me?"

"I don't presume to know which you'd prefer. Paid or not. I always just find someone willing because why pay someone who's not into you when you can find someone who's hot for it and free." She shrugged. "But I'm not judging. They have a union and great benefits here so..."

"They?" I interrupted.

"The prostitutes."

I blanched. "Seriously?"

"This is where I used to come get a lot of my..." She chewed her lip. "But I'm not here for that. I really thought you'd enjoy it."

I nodded once, not sure if I should believe her or not.

"So wander, go buy something. Whatever you want, it's on me."

If only I could actually let loose. I would kill for one more night before I was forced into picking the future queen. "I think I'll just get a drink and watch."

She scrutinized me. "I know you're gay Louis, so if you're avoiding a hook up because you think I don't know." She shrugged again. "Pointless."

I coughed. "What? How?"

"It's been obvious since we were kids. Like your obsession with Justin Timberlake was normal." She looked at the ceiling. "And it's a lot less likely you'll get recognized here. So you might as well blow your load as much as possible, get them to sign NDAs, and have your fun."

"You can't be serious. Our people are much more accepting."

"Sure, fine, that may be true. But here you don't have the Queen and Parliament to deal with. They might not even know it's against the Church of England to marry the same sex."

"I'm not sure it is, but it's still just not done. This was easier when you thought I was straight."

They both laughed at me. Women.

Elle was giggling next to her. "I'm pretty sure he thought I was for him."

"Seriously?" Anne looked horrified. "I don't give my

friends as sexual gifts to my brother." She turned to Elle. "Can you imagine?"

Elle laughed again. "He'd run me off before the week was out."

"No kidding." Anne laughed. "Get yourself some dick and leave my friends alone."

"Even if you know, I don't think I can—you know—perform knowing you might be watching, so I'll stick to my plan of spectating."

"I am going to stick to the first level after I say hi to Ben. You can have the other three, since I'm sure it's too crazy down there for your liking, and then come get me when you're done."

I groaned to myself. The possibilities were endless. I could sleep with half a dozen guys in a couple of hours. I could have a threesome. Who doesn't have a threesome fantasy? My cock was throbbing, and I needed to calm the fuck down. So I took a better look at my surroundings. This was as good a place as any to start, and if it wasn't, I wasn't above paying for it. I needed to fuck, and I hadn't realized how much until that very moment, but now I was going to be a man on a rampage because it had been near six months since I'd let myself loose.

LOUIS

I was on the edge of reaching the pinnacle of my sex life, and I held myself back. I was having a hard time convincing myself this wasn't a good idea. I needed to take a breather, and a drink was in order. My sister was still on this floor, and it wasn't gentlemanly to just drop trousers and go to it. I had some dignity, even as sex starved as I was. I would take my time. We had the rest of the night, well, until this establishment closed, so there was no reason for a rush.

I held out my wrist to the bartender and asked for a gin and tonic. He set it in front of me, and I surveyed the room. This would be a spectacular place to frequent if it were anywhere in London. Even if I didn't act on my needs, it was fascinating to watch people in their most primal state, and deep down I was a voyeur. I loved to watch. Or maybe it was the desire to be watched, and I was envious of those around me. I shouldn't even think those thoughts. I would never be allowed.

I made myself return to the hunt. My gaze roamed the interior of the bar. There weren't many people on this floor. It was exclusive, but not in a way I would have imagined. It had to be reserved for people the owner knew.

A figure in the shadows drew my attention. Most of the bar was dimly lit, but he'd picked the one spot barely visible. He sat slumped over his drink, shoulders hunched forward, and his head tipped down, like he was going to see something in the glass. Maybe his salvation waited at the bottom. He watched but from under the cowl of his hood. Had I not been firmly planted in reality, I would have suspected he was a damn wizard from Harry Potter, which would have been more fun than even this club. Or even a Jedi. I was starting to think this club was a stranger place than my sister let on. I wanted to know what the deal was with his hood. It seemed to be the last thing to wear in a club with the sole purpose of getting people high and laid. I already wanted to know his story, but he'd built an invisible wall around himself, so I wasn't sure he'd even talk to me.

The mystery was made clear moments later as he leaned into the light to speak to the bartender. He wore a scar from the middle of his forehead, through his eyebrow, curved across his cheek, and down into a ruined top lip. There was the hint of the scar apparent on his bottom lip like he'd kissed the blade at the end of its cut. It was lovely. He'd probably been model breathtaking beforehand, but now he was different. Otherworldly even. He had bronzed skin which faded to pale white along the scar and piercing slate coloured eyes. I couldn't stop staring, which was entirely rude of me, and probably what the man was used to, but for quite different reasons.

He looked up at me. There was such intensity in his gaze.

I couldn't look away, and he seemed intent on staring me down, making me feel ashamed for daring to be caught looking at him, but I wasn't backing down. My mind was made up. I had to talk to him. It was evident he wasn't happy to catch me and would probably tell me to fuck off, but something made me circle the bar to get closer to him.

I'd been told I was charming, so I tried to use it to my advantage, even if I was rusty.

"Can I buy you a pint?"

He looked me over as I moved towards him. "Sure, why not?" His American accent was charming, so much different than what I was used to.

He pulled further back into the shadows, probably hoping I hadn't noticed his scar.

"Put his on my tab, and I'll take another."

The bartender again scanned my bracelet which was still odd but better than putting a sex club on my credit card. "This system is better than dealing with the money here."

"Having trouble figuring it out?" he asked, looking slight amused.

I was in.

"It's all the same colour and size. How do you pay for anything drunk?"

There was the barest hint of a smile on his lips. "We use the numbers."

"I can pay for anything by size alone."

"You don't have to do this." He looked at me out of the corner of his eye.

"What do you mean?" I asked. I didn't know what he was getting at.

"Buy me a drink because I caught you staring." The way he pronounced even simple things got me going.

"I don't see that stopping you from drinking it," I retorted.

"I'm not rich enough to ever turn down a free drink." He took another pointed sip. "But the point remains, you don't have to pretend to be friendly."

"Wasn't why I bought you a drink." I paused to let the words sink in before going on. "And you're assuming I was staring for the wrong reason."

He brought his fingers to his scarred lip and scoffed. "They all say as much."

As jaded as he was, I wanted my sentiment to come through as genuine, and his rebuff only made him hotter. What did it say about me that rejection turned me on? Maybe it was exhilarating because I was never turned down, so being a nobody here in this bar made the chase all the better.

"I can assure you I was staring because you're lovely."

He turned to look at me, really look at me. It gave me a better view of his face as he leaned forward, and my opinion hadn't changed, in fact, between his skin tone and his eye colour, seeing him in the light made me more attracted to him. He had this intense look, something hardened into him. Nothing came easy to him, and he was willing to fight the world for it. Whatever had happened to him must have been at a young age, changing the rest of his life.

"Do I know you?" He narrowed his eyes, looking at me harder. "Are you here a lot?"

"No, first time."

He gasped and sat back. "You're him."

I scrubbed a hand over my face. "So much for anonymity."

He grabbed my hand and pulled it off my face, an intimate gesture, and it surprised me. "Don't cover your face."

He leaned closer, which bought colour to my cheeks.

"I'm sure you've seen enough pictures of me. Why the examination?"

"You're better looking in person. Maybe it's all those horrid uniforms and such they parade you around in."

"Pardon?"

"Those hideous blocks of red clash terribly with your red hair." He made a face, and I was offended.

"They don't clash with my hair." I ran my fingers through my auburn hair, wondering if he was right.

"Little bit."

"And what authority are you?"

He laughed. "I take photos for a living, so I have some authority on the matter."

"What industry do you work in?" As I said the words, I wasn't sure I wanted the answer.

He pulled back his lips and grimaced. "You don't want to know."

"Now you must tell me."

"I'm an independent contractor."

There was something he wasn't saying. "So like high fashion, magazines?"

"I guess you'd call me paparazzi."

Hell. "Just my luck. You have a fine evening." I slid off my stool, needing to go find some women to hit on or this would be all over the rags.

He grabbed my arm again, his fingers biting into my flesh this time. Clearly the man had no personal boundaries. "I signed the same NDA you did. Ben would have my balls if I published anything, and I don't write articles, I just take pictures. He has a moratorium for a block around the building."

"I can't." I pulled, but his fingers tightened.

"Can't what?"

"No," I whispered when I wanted to say yes. I wanted him to keep his hand on me.

He stood. "Can't have even a whisper?" He brushed his thumb over my wrist, entirely gentle considering what the rest of his fingers were doing.

"There is nothing to be talked about." My heart was hammering in my ears. If he said anything, if word got back to the Queen, I'd have to marry instantly.

"What did you mean when you called me lovely?"

"You are." I couldn't crush the man.

He used his free hand to drag the hood off his head. "Were you just saying that to be nice?"

I couldn't stop staring at him. "No," I said in a whisper, and I felt like a coward for the first time in my life. I'd told myself all the reasons I stayed in the closet, and most of them were for my country, but here standing before this lovely man they all felt like lies.

He stepped into my space, only a breath between us. "Do you usually call other men lovely?"

"Of course, all the time." I tried to laugh it off, but truth be told, if he got any closer he'd be able to feel for himself what I meant.

"So you don't want to find a private room?" He pressed into me, and I didn't pull back. He was as hard as I was. I was so worked up, and to get the fantasy dashed. I whimpered because he had me.

"I can't."

"I'll sign whatever you want." He grabbed a hold of my shirt, holding me in place, but he didn't need to. I wasn't going anywhere.

"Bloody hell." It was getting hard to get a full breath. I was pretty sure all the blood in my body was now circulating in my dick. "But you'll know. And you can look for me. An NDA does me no good if someone is on my trail."

"I don't work in the UK. I'm a gay man. I wouldn't out someone who didn't want to be outed. I do have scruples."

"A paparazzo with morals?" I wanted to laugh, to step back, to run my fingers through my hair, like the situation wasn't affecting me.

"We aren't all bad." He brushed his fingers over my bulge. I hadn't realized he'd let go of my wrist.

Hell. Fucking hell. "Where?" I was an idiot, and I knew this was going to come back to bite me in the ass, but I needed this. I was giving up my entire life for my country, and I deserved this.

His ruined lips curled in to a smile, and fuck I was smitten. "I have just the place."

He dragged me by my shirt, and I went willingly.

LOUIS

Since I was doing this, I was doing it. His body was hard and warm, and he was the most beautiful creature I'd ever seen. My chances to be stupid were fading, and I needed this, which would subsequently be the name of my autobiography when all this came out in the papers, but I'd already convinced myself with excuses of deserving it.

I pushed at his clothes as we stumbled towards wherever he was taking us. Where we were had left my mind, replaced by only need for human contact from this beautiful stranger. I traced my fingers over his abs and popped the button on his jeans. I had no excuses. I'd had barely more than a single drink, but I was drunk on exhilaration.

His hands wandered just as much as mine did, and when he pushed me through a door, I was ready. The door he'd opened was well concealed in the wall and opened with a press. A perk of knowing the owner? I was starting to wonder how much time the guy spent here, but as I didn't know his name and we were both here for the same thing, I wasn't about to ruin it with questions. I also found myself trusting the guy. A strange feeling indeed.

He kicked the door closed behind himself, leaving us alone in a dimly lit room. There was a sofa and a shower, and there were no other words to describe it but quaint. I wouldn't have wanted to take a blacklight to the place either, but when you were desperate. Once in the room he slowed down, taking his time kissing me. I was a starved man and I needed more, so I shoved my hands in the back of his trousers.

He dug his fingers into my bicep. "Not yet. I plan on enjoying you."

He pushed me back towards the sofa, and I went willingly. Maybe horizontal we would lose some clothes. He shoved me rather aggressively, and I fell back into a seat. I kicked my boots off as he dropped to his knees. Now we were talking. I could not wait to watch his lips on me. I learned forward to tug his shirt off.

"I'm going to leave that on, thanks."

Strange, but as he was unzipping my pants, my attention was elsewhere, and it was forgotten the moment my cock was exposed. My hips bucked involuntarily into his grasp as he closed his warm fingers around my length. I almost didn't recognise the sounds coming from my mouth.

"It has been awhile for you, hasn't it?"

"It's not easy to find dick when you're who I am."

"I bet it's easy to find dick, it's the keeping it a secret that can't be," he said and ended the conversation by pressing his lips to me.

My knees fell open, and I dropped my head back to rest against the sofa. He took me in an inch at a time, slowly, so fucking slow, when I wanted fast. I slid my fingers into his hair, unconsciously trying to urge him, but he resisted. Instead he pulled back and licked at the underside of my head.

"So used to getting everything you want."

I picked up my head to look at him there, hovering over my cock. "A little."

"The spoiled prince." He snapped his teeth, and if I hadn't been sitting, I would have jumped. "I guess I'll have to try and teach you patience in one night."

"I'm not going to like this, am I?"

"No, you're going to love it."

He took me fully into his mouth, and I believed him. In moments he had me panting and gripping the cushions, trying not to lose it. He swallowed around me, and I was pretty sure I saw the face of God in lights and colours behind my eyelids.

He came up smiling at me. His hair was tussled from my hands, and he was a smug bastard. "You're entirely too easy."

My cock was pulsing, begging for him to continue touching me, but I had a little dignity left in me. "It has been a rather long time, as I told you."

"Hmmhmm." He sat back on his heels. "Strip for me. I want to watch."

I wasn't sure why I did what he said, but again it was hot, and I was going to ride this out as long as possible and enjoy it. So I got to my feet and took my time undressing myself. I undid the buttons to my waistcoat one at a time and slid it off my arms, folding it and setting it aside before I moved on to my shirt. It was perfectly tailored to fit tight across my arms and chest. I worked hard for the body I had, in all the time I had not getting laid. What better way to work off sexual frustration?

He ate it up, finally looking as starved as I was, moving his gaze down my chest. My jeans sat low on my hips, and I pushed them down and stripped them off, also folding them.

"Not used to undressing yourself, are you?"

I laughed. "I always dress myself."

"I like it better my way." He was rubbing his hand over his dick through his jeans, and I couldn't take my eyes off of it. "I like the way you look at me."

"You're lovely. I can't help it." I reached out, needing to touch him, but he stepped back.

"I want you inside me."

I groaned. "You better have a condom."

He held one up and one of those individual packages of lube. He'd done this before, and I envied his freedom.

"You're going to have to lose some of those clothes." I put my hand over his, which he let me do. We stroked over his cock together as I kissed him.

He parted my lips and skimmed his tongue over mine. I gripped the back of his head, needing him to stay right where he was, a little afraid he'd try and back away again.

He did pull back, but not far. He looked me in the eyes. "I like kissing you."

"And I you." I tried for the button on his jeans, and this time he let me.

He looked at me with doubt in his eyes, and I wondered how many times he'd been rejected to have that so firmly in his mind. I kissed him again so he'd get the point.

Once his trousers were down around his ankles I tried again for his shirt, but he wasn't having it. I supposed it had something to do with the scar, maybe a continuation of it down his chest? Or maybe something worse.

I wanted to see it, but how, if our night was going to come to an end so quickly? It wasn't like things continued after an anonymous hook up. I didn't even know his name. Even as he pressed his body to mine, the thought stayed in the back of my head.

He closed a hand around our dicks and rubbed over us. "Where do you keep going?" he asked like my mind was bared open to him.

"I want to know what's under your shirt." I slipped my fingers under the hem, bushing them over his abs.

"I have to show my face, but I don't have to show my chest," he said over my lips.

"I'm sorry," I said, unsure why.

"I actually believe you." He looked into my eyes. "And I'm almost sure if we kept seeing each other I'd show you, but it's not in the cards for us."

He was giving me little pieces of himself. Pieces he probably didn't give anyone, and it was almost hotter than his hand on my cock.

"And I'm sure you're even more lovely with your shirt off." I scratched my nails down his chest before removing my hand. "Now turn around."

His lips turned up. "I think I like you bossy."

LOUIS

I woke up sober with a man in my bed. It was a first. Usually, I had to be pretty drunk to even consider risking it. I rolled to my back and stretched. It was nice to wake up to someone. They still did the separate room thing at the palace, which probably wouldn't change when I became king. Privacy would be nice while I was ghosting. Maybe I'd find a woman who would understand her role as my beard and take being rich and being the Queen over being in love. The thought turned my stomach. It wouldn't be a great thing, what I was doing, but the thought of the kind of woman who was just after my title and money made me cringe. Although, I really couldn't talk as I would be marrying for all the wrong reasons as well.

My mind, being the terrible place it was, started to imagine the ways I'd have to conceive an heir. I could use a turkey baster and no one would notice, right? I laughed a little too loud, and he started to stir next to me, and at that moment I realised I had no idea what his name was. Well, this was rather embarrassing. He obviously knew who I was, and I'd shagged him more than once, and never asked for his name.

I had a fun morning to look forward to. I was sure any moment Doug was going to bust in here and yell at me for ditching him last night, and after that I could ask the nice gentleman to write his name I didn't know on the nice NDA. Talk about hitting it out of the park.

I scrubbed a hand down my face. It was time to make some tea and face reality. I threw the covers off myself and sat, my feet finding the slippers placed there by the hotel staff the night before at some point. I shoved my feet into them and was about to stand when fingers found my wrist and yanked me back.

"Don't get up yet," he muttered in a sleepy voice.

I looked back over my shoulder. He lay there, his top half still in a shirt, with his hair tussled. His lips were parted, and the way he looked at me, I would have agreed to stay in bed with him all day.

"And why shouldn't I get up?" I asked.

"You don't enjoy morning sex?"

I'd actually never been allowed the delight. When I dared to indulge in one night stands, I was never at the palace, and when I was sneaking out, Doug was cleaning up the mess. Not an action that usually brought on the sexy. I cringed at the thought. It was all so clinical, and I was sorry I had to be that person.

"I can't say I've ever had the pleasure."

"Never?" He pulled again at my arm, and I gave in and laid back down.

"I'm sure you can imagine how my lifestyle wouldn't

permit it."

He closed his eyes, smiling. The light hit his face just right, highlighting the pale scar. It pulled when he stretched his lips, making his smile crooked. I wanted to see how his lips looked stretched around my dick. It had been too dark last night. I was going to hell, but I was going to enjoy it.

"What's in your head? You're making a face."

"I was thinking about how your lips would look wrapped around my cock."

He pressed his eyes closed. "You really want to see that?"

"Why wouldn't I?" I flipped my hand and broke the grip he had on my wrist and captured his, so I could move his fingers to my hard on. "I quite like the visual."

His smile broadened. "This doesn't bother you." He gestured at his face. "In the dark it's not so bad, but in the light…"

I leaned forward, brushing our lips together. "It's what drew me to you."

"You said that." He pulled a face and moved back. "But why?"

"Because I find it sexy."

Doubt filled his face. "You can't be serious."

"Could I have fucked nearly any bloke in that bar?"

He shrugged and nodded. "Yeah, and?"

"I wanted you."

"Or you were sex starved and I was just the first guy you saw."

"It had been months. I'm sure I could have gone fifteen more minutes."

He narrowed his eyes and tried to hide his smile. "Either

that or you were at critical mass and would have exploded if you didn't get laid right then."

"As I remember, I exploded a few times, but none of them were rushed."

He groaned and closed his fingers around my cock. "No, you're anything but a minute man."

"Precisely." He captured my mouth in a kiss before I could make any more points to my case.

It worked to my advantage that we were both still naked, and I took hold of his dick and matched his strokes, quite content to enjoy the slow build while our hands wandered.

"How were you picturing it?" he asked.

"What?" I was a little dazed by pleasure and wasn't sure what he was referring to.

"My lips around your cock. Was I on my knees or?"

"No." I wasn't ashamed to admit what my fantasy had been. "I was kneeling over your chest."

"So you like control? I knew I had you pegged right away as bossy."

"At times."

He flipped to his back. "Come on then."

I could have come right there, just looking at him laying like that waiting, but I wasn't about to miss the opportunity. I was going to need a lot to fill my spank bank for the dry years to come. I carefully straddled his torso and pressed my dick down with one hand to brush my tip over his lips. He parted them ever so slightly.

"Is this new for you too?"

"Just about everything that isn't a rushed quickie is," I said. I probably should have lied, instead of giving him more fodder to use if he decided to not sign the NDA, but at this very moment I couldn't bring myself to care. No wonder Doug insisted they sign them first.

He flicked his tongue over the tip of my head. "I can think of plenty of things you need to try before I let you out of this room then."

I pushed more of my dick into his mouth, because if I didn't shut him up, I was going to be a minute man. Which would have been more of a reason for the NDA than anything else. I could see the tabloid headlines. I shuddered in horror, not wanting to be the quick draw king. I also didn't want to think about the ways in which I wanted to keep him in the room. It wouldn't take much persuasion to keep me holed up here, and then how would that look to my grandmother?

He must have taken my shudder as something good because he grabbed my ass with one hand and forced my cock deeper in his throat. I really wasn't objecting, and it pushed everything else from my mind.

"Like that?" I asked him.

His eyes met mine, and it was everything. Watching him take me in and swallow around me. Complete submission in this position. His started to use his nails. My ass was going to be covered in marks, and it spurred me on until I was fucking his mouth with abandon. His eyes were wide, and his pupils dilated. I leaned forward, gripping the headboard, forcing the last inch of myself into his throat. He took it like a pro and swallowed around me, and I completely lost it like a barbarian. I was too awash in pleasure to do a thing about it. No warning, I just blew my load straight down his throat. I shook with the intensity of it.

His eyes glinted, and he licked me clean before I fell off him to the bed. I lay there panting like I'd just run a marathon. He laughed as he wiped his mouth with the back of his hand and rolled to his side.

"Daymn boy."

"I'm exceedingly sorry." I dared not look at him. I could hear him still laughing.

"What are you sorry for?" He brushed his fingers down my arm.

"Just letting loose like that. No warning."

"Were you going to give me a heads-up?"

"Yes."

"Umm why?"

I didn't understand his confusion. "It's generally considered rude to just come in someone's mouth. Not everyone is a fan."

He burst out laughing. "If your dick is in my mouth, I have a pretty good idea from experience what happens."

"I was trying to be polite."

"That's a thing with your people, isn't it?"

"Yes, I would say we are a polite society."

"Well I'm a dude and an American. If I have a dick in my mouth, I'm trying to get my partner to orgasm, and I know what that comes with. Now, had I said something about hating cum, which I don't, then it would be different."

"I concede your point, to a point."

He raised his brows, and I could tell he wanted me to enlighten him.

"It's never wrong to err on the side of caution."

"Try living dangerously, your highness. If even for a little while before you have to be king." I didn't know how those words would haunt me later, but they were forgotten for the moment as he took ahold of his dick, which distracted me from what we were talking about. "Now are you going to repay the favor?"

"God yes." I slid down in the bed until I was face to face with his magnificent cock.

"You're not afraid of cum are you?"

"Hardly."

"Is that permission to come in your mouth?"

"See, it isn't that hard to be a little polite."

He cock smacked me, ruining any of the attention of his request, but it made me so hard for him.

XAVIER

I watched as he showered. I wasn't ready to get up, but he insisted he needed to get going before his staff came looking for him. I could see where that would get dicey so I let him get out of bed instead of enticing him into more sex.

We were in the nicest hotel suite I'd ever seen. This wasn't a room a mere mortal could book. These were the rooms they kept back for celebrities and well— kings. The shower was big enough for an orgy and had probably seen quite a few of them. It was all glass with the shower head in the ceiling raining down over the occupant. I personally hated them, as it was like a constant rainstorm where you couldn't keep the water out of your face, but it was something to watch the water drip down the tight cords of his tanned muscular body.

He looked like a shampoo ad. He'd spent quite a few years in the Royal Air Force, and it had paid off. It would really be something to watch him work, and I didn't mean the hand holding and the ribbon cutting. I meant actually flying or PT or something akin. It was too bad it had to end. I used to hate the royals and the entire business of it. Sure, they served their purpose and got the ribbon cutting crap done so the Prime Minster could focus on governing in a way the American president couldn't, but the idea of someone being born into money and titles makes my skin crawl.

I had a hard enough time with the billionaire class in my own country. It was really no different. At least some of the billionaires earned their money, even if there was a crooked system of rich welfare keeping all their money in their pockets. Call me cynical, but I was a realist. But he was somehow different than I'd expected. Too good. It was surreal and threw off all the ingrained perceptions I'd had of his type.

Beside his personality, knowing what I now knew, it was impossible to keep hating him. Sure he had everything handed to him in life and every opportunity, but as forward as the UK was, far ahead of the US in gay rights, the monarchy was still stuck in the last century. It wasn't too long ago a king had to abdicate for wanting to marry a divorcee. I couldn't imagine the scandal it would cause if Louis was outed, and there really wasn't a better option. As I understood it, his younger sister was an addict who had a hard time staying sober, but she was probably more qualified in the eyes of the church of England than the gay guy, which was just sad.

So I had feelings, and I generally tried not to have feelings. Life was easier without feelings, and my job would be impossible if I felt bad about things.

"Er...are you sure you don't want to join me?"

"You don't know my name, do you?"

"You never told it to me."

He was right, but I was still going to give him no end of shit for it. "You have a guy's cock in your mouth and your dick in his ass and you didn't even bother to get a name? And you claim you never do this."

His whole body language changed, and he looked genuinely concerned like he'd deeply wounded me. I couldn't help it. I burst out laughing.

"What is your name?" He had his hands on his hips now and his toothbrush sticking out of his mouth. If only I could shoot this. Not even to sell the pictures, even though they would be worth a fortune, but for the memories. No one got the prince this way. Not even his wife would see this rare glimpse into who he really was. I loved seeing people in their raw form. I couldn't help it.

"Xavier. You can call me X, most do."

"It's a pleasure to make your acquaintance, Xavier."

"You can't turn that off, can you?" I flipped to my back, throwing the covers off and sprawling out naked from the waist down, all over his sheets.

"No, it's quite impressive programming." He took quite a notice, and I loved the affect I had on him.

It was thrilling. I got my fair share of hookups using apps by displaying my lower half, but most people took issue with my ruined face, and there weren't many second dates, and if there was a second, it was usually out of pity. I didn't have time for pity.

"It's rather impressive, and if we were friends, I'd have a good time abusing it."

"If?" he asked.

"We're hardly friends. We just met." I laughed, wondering

how hard it was for the guy to make genuine friends. He probably didn't have many, if any.

"We could be."

"Are you looking for a fuck buddy, my dear prince?"

He knit his brow, and I could tell I'd offended him. "I meant it as I said it. I would never presume to use you as such."

"You don't have to take everything so poorly." I slid out of the bed, deciding I should take him up on the offer for a shower.

"It would be impossible for us to be fuck buddies. You live here."

"And friendship would be easier?"

"I have a phone," I said, a little sad. He would be fun to play with all soapy and wet.

"I'm shocked they allow you people to have phones." I slapped my cheeks and mocked surprised.

He scoffed at me. "I'm actually surprised too, as it's more trouble than not."

"I'm not surprised. I'm imagining Snapchat getting leaked."

"Screenshots of entire conversations are leaked. It can be a nightmare."

I chuckled to myself, imagining what was on Louis' phone. "I'd be amused if they'd ban you guys from it."

"We are already banned from social media." He'd finished the brushing and moved to using a bar of soap so erotically I was a bit jealous.

"I couldn't possibly join you. I can smell your bath soap from here."

"Why would that prevent you from joining me?"

"I can't go to work smelling like the garden of Eden."

"Not manly enough to own smelling nice? Tis a shame."

I glared at him. "There a difference between smelling good and coating your body in the entire contents of Bath and Body Works."

"You didn't seem to mind when my cock was in your mouth."

He had a point, and I was at a loss for words. He turned his back to me, and maybe it was I who wanted the fuck buddy relationship over friendship. It was impossible, but a guy can fantasize right? I was sure going to commit as much of this as I could to memory.

"Look at you watching."

He'd turned back around, and I'd hardly noticed. I was thankful my pigment didn't allow for my embarrassment to show.

"The whole world looks at you, and you don't think I'm going to enjoy it while I have it."

He didn't say anything. He just stared at me with those intense eyes as he stepped out of the shower. I couldn't look away. I was going to be sad when he left. This was the best sex I'd had in years.

"Put your number in here." He handed me his phone after he'd tossed his towel aside, still completely in the nude. He was comfortable in his own skin, and I liked that. "I'm sorry I have to be getting ready. Previous engagements and all."

"Canada, huh?"

"Of course, otherwise I'd still be in bed with you." He'd started to dress himself, and I flipped around in bed to watch.

"You're taking great pleasure in this, aren't you?"

"How could I not?"

He slipped on a pair of bespoke pants, and I wanted to take them back off him. The way his hips cut into them. It was spank bank material for life. Even the way he buttoned up his shirt was regal. He added suspenders, and I was groaning. He shot me a warning look.

"What?"

"You're making it difficult for me to be on time."

"So don't be."

He growled. Actually growled at me like he was some primal animal.

"It's important to be punctual."

I rolled to my back, letting my head hang off the end of the bed so I could still see him, while he got a good look at where my hand was going.

"You arse."

"I freelance. I don't have anywhere to be."

His eyes narrowed. "Now you're going to have me thinking about you here while I'm visiting a hospital."

"Shame." I curled my fingers around myself.

His eyes were glued to my dick. "Being half hard on public visits is frowned upon."

"Then maybe you should find a bathroom to relieve yourself while thinking of me."

His eyes pressed closed, and there was pure sex written all over his face. He gripped himself and groaned again. "I think I will."

And I knew I'd remember that image of him for the rest of my life. And I used it to get myself off after he left. There was a bodyguard and an NDA waiting when I opened the door to the room. Poor guy must have been standing there awhile. I'd taken my time enjoying the shower. I signed, because I knew what he was, and I didn't want him to worry. We'd never see each other again. Or so I thought until my phone started to ring.

XAVIER

Instead of going back to my loft and having a nice brunch and checking my email, I got the phone call from hell. What even were the odds? Okay, super high considering what I did for a living, but photographing the guy I'd just fucked was going to be super awkward. 'Hey I know I just saw you naked, but act like you don't know me so you can stay in the closet while I take your picture okay?'

No. Nope. There was no way I could. It wouldn't be right.

"You have to take the job."

"I work freelance, and…" I was out of excuses. What could I possibly say? Even me telling Eran I'd fucked the dude wouldn't get him off my case. I needed to make up an excuse to go to Barbados to stalk Heidi Klum or something.

"X, all my other guys are on vacation, and I need a picture of this girl. There are rumors they were at a sex club."

I dropped my phone, and there it went skidding across the icy sidewalk and got kicked by some dude stepping off the subway stairs. I would be lucky if it wasn't shattered to five million pieces. I went running after it, my mind spinning in a thousand different directions.

Someone had broken the NDA, and Ben was going to be pissed. This was already too close to home. I'd signed an NDA, and I didn't want to be wrapped up in this mess. What if I got banned from the club and sued at the same time? I picked up my phone before it was kicked again and put it back to my ear, happy it was still in one piece.

"A sex club?" I said when I realized he was waiting for me to reply. I hoped I sounded shocked enough.

"Where have you been? Did you not hear me? This is big. The pictures could be worth a fortune."

"Got bumped into on the street and dropped my phone." I inhaled the icy air. "Not a fortune if you're paying me to be there. I'm sure it's a flat rate." I knew the drill, which is why I preferred to work as a contractor.

"You know I'm paying for expenses, and there will be a sizable bonus if you get something."

Why had I answered the phone? "I don't know."

"You never waffle on me. What's going on?"

Shit. He was on to me. There was no way I was getting out of this now. Eran had worked in the business for a long time, and he was damn good at reading people. It's how you get as far as he has.

"I know you like working for yourself, but when I've thrown a lead and money at you in the past you've always jumped at it..." he trailed off. I had to get him off the scent.

"He's not even staying in Chicago, so how much of this sex club rumor is going to play a factor? And it's fucking cold in Canada." I hoped it was enough.

"The guy has never had a girlfriend. Never been photographed with a woman, and clearly he makes all the girls he sleeps around with sign ironclad NDAs, so all we get is whispers. A photo of him with someone...Come on, think about it."

He'd never been photographed with a woman because he liked cock, but I couldn't say it, not that I would, even had I not signed the NDA. "You're right. It could be huge if he's actually seeing someone."

"And didn't you see the news?"

"What news?" Had I missed something? I racked my brain. Royals weren't really my thing. I pretty much kept to celebrities in my country.

"A source close to the Queen is saying she told him he needs to pick someone to marry when he gets back. This could be the start of it. What if you get a picture of the future princess?"

"What's all this about the club?" If I could give Ben a heads-up, I was going to. He'd always done me a solid with his club.

"Shit, get this. I've been told the place is also a drug and prostitute front set up like a secret club, and the Chicago police are ass deep in it."

"You know I'm not an investigative reporter."

"I've got someone else on it, don't worry, but I do want Princess Anne followed. I mean, if you could get pictures of her or hell even the Prince going into one of these places?"

"This isn't my usual gig."

"So when you blew open a certain socialite going for

plastic surgery that wasn't like this?"

I sighed. It wasn't different. I mostly liked getting the photos of people on dates and such. "That photo paid off my condo."

"Believe me, I know. If you recall, I lost the bidding war." He laughed.

"Fifty K more is fifty k." He knew it was business just like I did.

"So tell me you'll do it. We have a right to know what these people are getting up to on their people's dime. It's social justice."

I didn't agree with him. A lot of my job was what I could reason out with my own morals. Everyone was entitled to a private life. I was never going to be the guy using a long-range lens to get naked photos of celebrities in their house, but in public I was all about it. "If it's a public place…"

"Hidden in plain sight, I'm told. All I need is a photo of them going in to one of these joints." He paused before going on. "Or a picture of him with this chick."

"If I get something, I'm going to need you to show me the green." It was probably wrong for me to think of getting to see Louis again. He'd probably never talk to me again anyway.

"You need to offer me an exclusive then."

If only he knew. "Send it to me in writing and what you're willing to pay."

"That a boy."

I hung up the phone, feeling a little slimy.

XAVIER

I bought the biggest, fluffiest, marshmallow looking coat I could find before getting on the flight Eran had booked for me, and I was still an icicle when I got off the plane. There wasn't enough maple syrup donuts in the world to justify this. I was on my third cup of Tim Horton's coffee before I spotted Louis, and despite all the hype, it was like crack.

I could not handle the politeness or the accents. I was going to be the American cliché. Not only was I bursting out laughing every time someone said 'eh,' but I might as well have been draped in an American flag riding a scooter with sparklers on the back for as much as I looked like a damn tourist. There was a reason I liked to stick to my own country. Now I know why people from other countries hated us. I didn't speak a word of French and stared blankly nearly every time someone tried to talk to me. I needed to go pick up 'how to act Canadian for dummies' before I made more of an ass of myself.

The only saving grace had been Louis hadn't noticed me yet. I knew it was coming. I couldn't keep hiding in plain sight if I wanted to get the good photos, but I so wasn't ready. Eran kept bugging me to camp outside his hotel and see who he was going in and out with, but I couldn't bring myself to.

My days started and ended with Louis. I was there when he walked out of the building in the morning and when he returned. The first two days I followed him for his daily activities but quickly decided there wasn't a point. There where hundreds of photos of him from amateur photogs, as well as professionals on his staff paid to take their pictures at the events for distribution, and I was one of the pack that choose to follow them around.

Royalty were all the rage. I was just imagining screaming teenagers in my mind, thinking if they could get close enough to him he'd surely whisk them off their feet and out of their boring lives and they'd be like some Lifetime movie.

But those pictures weren't worth shit. Unless you caught the royals doing something wrong, it wasn't worth pennies. I would have been better off stalking celebrities which was my usual gig anyway. At least in the cities I worked in more often I knew the spots. I was hitting a wall. I was going to have to follow Eran's advice and start stalking his entrances and exits, but that also meant coming face to face with him again.

Eran worked his magic and got a copy of Louis' public schedule as well as his private one. Everything would be leaked for a price, and Eran had the money to make people talk. When I freelanced I had to front it all myself. It was nice to have a backer, but the payouts were never as high. Always a gamble, steady vs big checks and not knowing when the next one would be. He wasn't far off his schedule which was a good day for someone like him, rolling up only an hour after the listed time. I got to my feet and put my camera to my face as the black SUVs rolled to a stop at the back entrance to the hotel.

I hid behind the camera and prayed to any deity that would listen he wouldn't notice. I could image he was used to tuning out my kind, so I just needed a little damn luck. He stepped out of the car, and of course I was the only one there. The schedule had been leaked, but Eran must be the only one with it at this point, which was great for him and terrible for me staying anonymous.

I snapped away, willing him to keep talking to Anne. These pictures wouldn't be worth a dime, but I was getting paid to do this, and if there were people not on his staff with him, which I doubted as he'd been in bed with me only a few nights ago, then they'd be worth something. I could analyze them later and keep an eye on it.

My luck ran out there. Louis looked up at the flash and looked right at me. Not like it was easy to hide the giant telling scar on my face, which was probably visible from space. His eyes locked on me and he faltered, coming to a standstill, which of course caught the attention of everyone else around him. Anne looked around and spotted me. She tugged on his sleeve, asking him why he was staring. Like they hadn't had cameras in their face their entire life, I could imagine her line of thinking.

The bodyguard who I'd signed the NDA for did a double take and realized what was going on. The social sectary, distinctly noticeable by the book in her hand she was looking at while walking with glasses at the tip of her nose got almost to the doors before realizing she left everyone behind. She whirled around and took in the scene, clearly confused.

I was glad I was the only photog here, because this was a shitshow.

Louis blinked at me, and then seemed to remember himself. He plastered a smile on his face and put his head down, power walking towards the door. Once he and his team where safe inside, I slumped back against the wall. How the hell was I going to do this for the next month or however long Eran decided paying for this was worthwhile?

The next two days he didn't give me a second glance as he walked in or out of the building. I didn't blame him, but there was a part of me that wanted to explain it to him. To say something so he wouldn't hate me. I didn't want him to regret what we'd done and ruin it for him. He had my number and he wasn't using it, which pretty much spelled out how he felt about continuing the friendship like he said he wanted to. It was a line, and I should have known better.

I was so close to calling Eran and canceling this entire thing, but I couldn't come up with a good excuse. I couldn't come up with anything. I wanted to bang my head against a wall, a wall in my own damn loft and then hibernate for the next month. But instead I kept walking. My stomach was growling, and if I didn't fill it I wouldn't get in my afternoon nap before Louis returned to his hotel.

A car circled the block. I'd seen it before. There weren't that many blacked out SUVs in the city. I walked another block and saw it again. This time I took mental note of the license plate, and by the time I saw it a fourth time I knew I was being followed. It would be my luck for Louis to have put a hit out on me. As long as it was fast, he just needed to get it over with, but he'd probably want to torture me as well, which I might enjoy.

My mind was a fucked up place. After a few blocks, the same SUV started to keep pace. It couldn't be a coincidence. City traffic was rage inducing on its best days. There wasn't any meandering or scenic viewing in a blacked out and probably bulletproof vehicle.

So I stopped and turned to stare it down as I crossed my arms over my chest. "Let's do this." Not that they could hear me through the thick monstrosity, but hey I wanted to go out with some balls.

As I expected, they pulled over to the curb in front of where I stood. I waited. They could take all the time they wanted. I only had a prince to stalk in the evening hours, and from what I could gather from his press schedule, he was being shuffled from event to event in tight sequence. So this was probably just some palace lackey come to rough me up or throw around the NDA.

The window started to lower. "Bring it bitch," I muttered to myself and then was stuck speechless by the face starting back at me.

"Can we have a word?" Louis said through his teeth.

I'd really thought he was smarter than this. I looked up and down the street and then nodded. "This isn't a good idea."

A bodyguard stepped out from the front as I approached. He put a hand on my chest.

"You stalk me and think I'm going to kill you? Sure, just take the gun I carry around with me everywhere. You know how we Chicagoans roll."

"Is this really necessary?" Louis asked. "He doesn't have a gun."

"We're already in this because of your indiscretion the other night, Sir," he said the sir like there was tension there. "Do you think I should do my job, or do you want the paparazzi getting in here with a mic?"

"I was going to lunch and you found me. Everything I own except my wallet is in my room," I commented, but no one was listening to me.

But Muscles patted down every inch of me anyway.

"Those are my balls, not a mic, and he's already seen them."

The prince looked like he was going to have a panic attack.

Muscles growled and shoved me towards the back of the car.

"You were the one fondling," I said as I slid inside. This was probably the way I go, but maybe it would be worth it for one last taste.

"What the bloody hell?" Louis asked as soon as I had the door closed. "You can't just say those things in public."

"Then tell your suit not to touch my balls." I adjusted them. "He wasn't gentle."

"He's worked up because of you being here."

"And you think I'm not?" I glanced at the partition separating us from Muscles and was grateful. "Please enlighten me as to why you are following me so I can go get my lunch." I sat back to look at him.

His nostrils flared before he spoke. "We have an NDA."

Someone who didn't know him well wouldn't have

noticed, and I probably wouldn't except we'd spent time in bed and my job was to read people, but he was irate. It was written in the fabric of him. Laced through his muscles and the tightness in his neck. Even his hands flexed and unflexed. A tic he probably didn't even know he had. He didn't like to show it. He hid it well, more training I guessed.

"Sure we do."

"Then why are you here?" He was still doing the whole talking through a clenched jaw.

"My job. It wasn't by choice."

"Are you going to sit and give me the bare minimum?" He was entirely too used to getting his way. I bet men and women fell all over themselves to give him what he wanted, including information, making him deficient in dealing with an adversary.

"I was dragged into the back of a van, and I'm sure your plan was to beat me into submission. Do you expect me to bend the knee?"

His face tightened. "You drew me in hook and line, and now you're going to use it to get ahead."

"What do you think I'm going to use?"

"You knew where we were. Do you hang out there to see who you can catch?"

"Ben is my friend. I wouldn't breathe a word to anyone even if his NDA didn't make yours look like a joke. You think what they had you sign was long? This is my job. Ben likes me, but he likes his livelihood more. I didn't use you. We used each other."

"Still, you learn so much sitting there."

"Nothing I couldn't learn other ways. Everyone has

secrets."

"You're still missing the point. You lured me in."

"You hit on me." I was flabbergasted he'd turned this all around on me. "They were just lines you feed everyone, weren't they?"

"No," he said under his breath. He lifted his gaze to mine.

"Why didn't you just text me?"

"Why'd you take this job?"

I ground my teeth. "Saying no would have raised more red flags than taking the damn thing."

He shook his head and broke the eye contact. "I don't believe you."

"What do you want me to tell you? I got a call. They know about your sister going to Ben's. And they think you're dating someone. I got offered good money to come here, and when I started to say no he got suspicious. They didn't know you were there, which is lucky on your part. But between her drug issues and what was leaked about you having to get married, they want me to follow you both. Someone else saw her there. You're lucky we left when we did because we weren't seen, as that would be a much bigger story than me getting paid to be here for a few weeks following you around." My words got to him. I know they did. He was even more protective of Anne than his own image, but the ship had sailed on that one. If she was back into drugs, it would come out, like everything else. It always did.

His expression changed, first it was shock, and then he moved to rage, and if he was going to go off on me for telling him the truth, I was going to lose it. No, I'd just leave. This wasn't my world or my issue. I was taking pictures of their extracurricular activities, and that was it.

When he still hadn't answered, I put my hand on the handle. "We don't know each other from this point on. I meant what I said. I signed the NDA for a reason. I shouldn't have even told you what I was after because now I'm sure I won't get the picture I want, but whatever."

I didn't know what I wanted from him, but I surely wasn't about to get it, so I squeezed the handle and pushed against the door. It didn't budge. My eyes flashed back to his.

"Child locks?"

He scoffed. "Please, like they'd lock me in my own car. Doug is standing on the other side."

I crossed my arms over my chest. "Say your piece so I can go. I'm sure you're going to be missed before I'll be."

Brooding silence.

I dropped my head back to the glass. I liked the guy. I had, but now I wanted to slug him. His fingers slid up my thigh, and my head snapped up.

"Fancy a fuck?"

"What in the actual hell?" I was a little hard, don't get me wrong, but this was not the time or place.

"I have twenty minutes." He was loosening his tie with his free hand.

"You know who and what I am."

"Yes." His fingers stopped just short of my bulge.

I wanted him. I wanted to feel the way he made me feel. "We haven't done anything we can't take back." I tried. I stammered. I wanted to believe it myself.

"We've already done this." He was at my lips, a breath, no a whisper, would change it.

"This wouldn't be covered by our original NDA."

"You just gave me a big speech about how you're not out to get me."

"I'm not." And I really wasn't. "But how do you know I'll sign a second one?"

"I don't." He closed the distance, and he was warm and welcoming. He could feel so good. It would be so easy to give him what he wanted. I could forget myself in him for a while. But I couldn't.

My hand was between us, on his shirt, gripping it. Was I holding him there or pushing him away? I wasn't sure I knew. My body wanted it, but my mind was in rebellion. I had to let him go be him so I could keep being me. And it was entirely selfish. I didn't give a damn about his image. I couldn't. So I pressed, pressed him away, pressed him out of my life.

And as he panted, heavy breaths, breathing the same air I did. I said as much. "We don't know each other after this."

He looked hopeful, and I realized the fault in my words. "Right now. This moment. Nothing has happened. I was never here." And stupidly when he looked at me again I kissed him. I couldn't help it.

There was harmony in his lips and tongue. He even tasted regal, if that was a thing. I'm sure it was all in my intoxicated mind. I pushed again, and we broke apart, but instead of the gasping, his mouth was at my throat. Kissing my neck, seducing me with his lips.

I pressed back against the door. "We can't, because if we do we won't stop."

He groaned against my skin. Were there words? If so, I was more enticed by the sound than what he was saying.

"You want me."

"Yes." I wasn't sure if I spoke the word or thought it, but he certainly understood the gist. He pushed his hands under my shirt, and his skin on mine was almost too much. My will was cracking, and it would shatter, because it was him.

"You are not easy to say no to."

"Yes," he agreed before sinking his teeth in to my shoulder.

I kicked the floor, and my head hit the window. "We can't keep…" My words were lost in the exploration of his mouth, and I wasn't really sure where I was going with anything. My life choices all seemed to not make sense.

"There is no keep. We are here, why waste it."

My brain wanted to agree with him, but there was the nagging in the back, and I had to do… something? He grabbed my ass, and my fingers worked their way into his hair of their own accord.

"But it would be a keep."

"One for the road is all." He was working his way lower and getting on his knees.

I already knew how his tongue worked, and with the added image of him on his knees, it would be too easy to give into him. I would probably enjoy it more than he did, well, maybe as much. He was depraved by all accounts.

"I can't." I tightened my grip on his hair, preventing him from dipping any lower. "It's a conflict of interest." And the details of why this was a bad idea came flooding back. "I'm here on someone else's dime, and if I do this and sign an NDA with you. I can't."

He'd stopped, which saved me, because if he hadn't I

wasn't sure I could resist him much longer. My dick was already painfully hard, and he was him after all. He dropped his face to my lap and groaned. Not a sexual groan, an angry he knew I was right groan.

"I understand."

There was a tap on the divider, which probably meant he had to go anyway, and before I knew it I was out on the street like the fairytale had never happened.

XAVIER

I still wasn't right hours after the encounter, and I regretted not sleeping with him, but if I had we'd be down a rabbit hole of not stopping. Louis had an addictive quality, and he would be my drug of choice. I wasn't ready to be an addict, especially to someone as unavailable as he was. If I was getting addicted to something, damnit it was going be easy to obtain, like heroin or meth.

I sighed and leaned back against the back entrance of the hotel where they usually came out. I should take up smoking again. Now that was an addiction that would bring me some joy and then I'd have something to do with my hands with all this asinine waiting. I was starting to get fidgety, and I wasn't really happy about it. It had been a week of this, and tonight would probably be the same. Out for dinner someplace swanky where the chef would fall all over himself to show the royals a good time, ensuring his restaurant would be packed for months. I'd wait here then follow him and wait there. And this was my chosen profession. By accident sure, but I'd been doing it for a good five years now. Starting over as something else wasn't really appealing, especially since interviews didn't tend to work out for me.

I was starting to wonder where I'd gone wrong in life, everywhere, when his accent lured me from my trance.

"Still here, eh?"

"Are you adapting the slang?" I turned to look at him. "It's a little painful to listen to."

"Lord no, but it is contagious."

"What are you doing out here without your shields?" I wasn't bitter about the way he'd spent the last week surrounded by giant men so even if I wanted a lame picture of him leaving his hotel I couldn't get more than an elbow.

"They don't know I'm down here."

That got my attention. I stepped around the building and into the shadows with him, leaving my camera where it sat in my bag. "How'd you manage that?"

"I have my ways." He lowered his gaze down my form.

"The real question is why?"

"Bored."

"So you figured you'd come let me take your picture?"

"Hardly." He elongated the word, letting it roll off his sexy tongue, and I was sure it was for my benefit.

"What then?"

He locked his eyes back to mine and slowly shook his head. "Too easy."

"Easy?" He wanted to play games then. But why with me? Because I was dangerous.

"If I divulge anything, it could end up in print, so I will

mince my words."

I wanted to sigh at him, but I settled for a look. "I will repeat, I am not a reporter."

"I'm sure they'd buy tips." His beautiful mouth flattened to a line.

"Then why are you out here?"

He lifted a shoulder and shook his head.

"So it's gestures only now?" I signed he was a dumbass in ASL.

"You're signing at me?"

I scoffed. "You were the one who said you couldn't speak."

"Pretty sure sign language still counts, and how do you even know that shit?"

"My sister lost her hearing when we were kids."

He nodded like there was a shared something between us, and maybe there was.

"I can't stand you."

"Now you don't like me?" I asked.

"It's a complicated thing in my head."

"You were just trying to fuck me earlier. I guess I get why you do. There are plenty of jackasses I've wanted to hit for my sister."

"Now imagine if it was the entire world you had to fight."

"Okay, now you're getting a little vain."

He slid down the wall to sit against it. "You know what I mean."

I looked at him and squared down so we were on the same level. "I'd probably kill anyone who tried to post a picture of my sister she didn't want out there."

"And that's your job."

I shook my head. "I warned you, so give me some credit."

"I'm still not sure why you did."

I lifted my shoulder, mirroring his previous gesture. "Good question, but it was clear you weren't going back to Ben's, and I wasn't about to say anything about it to the guy who hired me."

"What if I went back?"

Was he testing me? My upper lip stiffened, but I forced it to relax. It was done and over.

"Wouldn't matter. I owe Ben my life, and like I said, to even get my ass in the door with the job I have the NDA made yours look like a joke."

"It was that bad?"

"Yup, and I enjoy not being bankrupt. On top of that, dude would fuck me up. There is a reason it's word of mouth only, and you have to have a recommendation to get in."

"Sounds like it was the safest place for Anne to hang out."

We fell into a comfortable silence. It wasn't awkward, but I still couldn't figure out what he was doing down here.

"You still interested in being friends?"

Well that caught me off guard. "There is no way that could work. It wasn't going to work when this wasn't my job. You have to be straight, and we couldn't even be in the car alone without us both wanting to fuck."

"You wanted to?" This seemed to please him.

"Of course I did. I'm just not stupid." Or I did my best not to be.

"I've been thinking about it."

I straighten back up and scrubbed a hand over my face.

"Have you now?" This was going to be rich.

"I have."

"You mean you're sex starved and you've been thinking about my cock." I turned back around and emphasized my point with my dick at his eye level.

He gave me a flat look. A sassy flat look. One only someone who was going to inherit a country could get away with. I bit back a laugh.

"No."

"I'm waiting."

He made me wait too, taking his sweet ass time. "You're different."

"You don't get out much, do you? I'm kind of a dick."

His brows rose, but he didn't take the bait. How hard was it to be this guy and watch everything you said around everyone because it was going to get back to the press or something?

"Come on," I coaxed, suddenly wanting to hear his explanation, not that I'd ever let on.

"You're not..." He paused and did the most god damn adorable thing I've ever seen in my life. He ruffled his own hair, then immediately started to smooth it back out like he realized it was a bad habit and was trying to correct it before anyone else noticed. I wondered if anyone else had ever witnessed the thing.

Getting this side of him was intoxicating because I knew no one else got to see it. Before today I would have had a hard time imagining Louis in casual clothes, sitting off the alley where the hotel took out it's garbage. It was one thing to exit this way to avoid my kind, but this was something else entirely.

"I'm not?" I prompted, when he didn't answer.

"I don't know how to word it without being offensive."

"It looks like you're going to have to be offensive."

He glared at me.

"Oh, right, you're too worried I'm going to write about it." I tapped my camera bag. "I take pictures. I don't interpret the pictures. I don't write the stories. I just take pictures in public places. I won't even do that shady vacation work bullshit with the high zoom lens. I have a few fucking principles."

He leaned his head back against the dirty wall. Trust was not a thing he possessed. He didn't know how. He'd been trained his entire life to be careful, and it'd left its mark. It was there to see. All the money in the world wasn't worth that to me. Maybe I was the lucky one with my disfigured face because even though people stared at me, I wasn't him. He couldn't get away from it, and all he had to do was be born.

"It's hard to believe you...your profession actually has scruples," he said carefully.

I was used to it. I'd been called all the worst names in the book. Yes, most famous people hated us, but they forgot they needed to thank us. "You know we are the reason most celebrities make as much money as they do. The more people want pictures the more they are worth in their respective jobs." Sure, Louis wasn't the same, but the press sold things and made the world go round. "Half the tips I get come from their publicists anyway, especially for the new type of reality TV celebrity types. You can't tell me I'm not feeding a need."

"This is something we aren't going to see eye to eye on."

"And with your life I don't blame you. But this is

something I'm really good at, and like I said, publicity sells more than just magazines."

He shrugged and looked back at the sky.

"Don't you have some place to be?"

He looked over at me almost lazily. "Dinner, but Anne is throwing a fit. She's been in a shit mood since I put a ban on any 'fun'." He made air quotes. "So she's refusing to go tonight."

"You're not asking me?"

He laughed. "No, even I'm not that stupid."

I held up my hands. "You never know. There are some pretty stupid people out there."

Back to silence. He was clearly deciding if he was going to say something and I was going to leave it. This wasn't my shit to work out, and I wasn't even sure he wanted to be talking to me. It was like a slim pickings situation. There was just no one else.

"Why are you so resistant to friendship?" he asked at last.

"I thought we went over this?" I tapped my chin. "Ah, yes, I remember. I was naked in your bed, you're the prince, and I'm the pauper."

"You don't even know what pauper means."

"It's British, it's enough."

He laughed.

"And worse, I'm the worst kind of person. My literal job is to take photos of you. Are you this dense in all aspects of your life? Because if you are, I fear for your country."

He held up his middle finger. "Look, I do know some sign language."

"I should get a photo of that just to teach you a lesson."

That got him to put it away real fucking fast. "You'd like to have something to hold over me, wouldn't you?"

I was not going to answer that. Damn I really couldn't because I'd go straight to the gutter if I did.

He nodded, so smug and self-assured. "I can see it in your eyes."

I held out my hands again, like he didn't phase me, but he did. Friends was bad because I'd want to fuck him again.

"Do you need to use your hands for expressions because your face is incapable?"

"I'm British. We don't use our faces. We are too posh." He was acting like he won. "Now, remind me why friends doesn't work."

"Why would you even trust me? You can't even speak openly in front of me. What would our friendship be like?"

"You haven't entered into the friendship agreement yet, so no I can't."

"Is this some magical wizard bond Harry Potter shit that once I enter into I'll die if I break?"

"It's not an unbreakable curse. But a gentleman's agreement."

"Does this involve another giant NDA?" I asked. I'd probably sign it if he asked, but then there wasn't really anything there.

As if he read my mind. "No, if I have to make you sign something to be my friend it's not real."

I nodded. "And why do you think you can trust me?"

"Ben does."

"You don't even know Ben." Was he stupid? Not that it wasn't true. I was trustworthy as fuck, but damn. He really was desperate, wasn't he?

"I can tell with you."

I raised a brow. "Tell what?"

"You're the type of man who keeps his word." There was so much faith in his line, and I wanted to be that person for him.

I was that person. I kept my word, but with him it was so much more. This would never be a friendship on equal footing, and could I just turn off my attraction for him? I didn't know.

"I'm not wrong, am I?"

"No." I couldn't leave it as my soft-spoken agreement. I have my dickish image to uphold. "You're just doing this to get me back into bed, aren't you? Need a fuck buddy to keep around?"

"I don't need to perpetrate a ruse to get you back into bed with me."

"Oh?"

"It would be easy." He stood and brushed off his jeans.

"Excuse me?" This guy was so confident it was bordering on unattractive, but it just made my dick harder for him.

"Yes."

"You think you could just get me back into bed?"

"I do." There wasn't even arrogance. He was just self-assured. Fucker was too used to getting whatever his royal ass wanted.

"I turned you down."

"Barely."

"How would you do it then?" I raised both my brows and crossed my arms over my chest.

He curled a finger at me. I moved closer almost against my

will.

"That would be telling." He smirked.

I scowled at him. "You have nothing." But maybe I believed he did have something up his sleeve. Or hell, maybe he could just tell I was hot for him. I clearly was. He knew what he did to people. I was just going to have to get better at ignoring it.

"Anne and I will be coming out the back at ten-thirty and we'll be going to Seven."

If I had been drinking something I would have spit it out. "Why are you telling me this?"

"Consider it repayment of information and a down payment on our friendship."

LOUIS

Was I daft? I probably was, and the mirror wasn't going to tell me a damn thing other than I looked good. 'Cute but stupid' would be printed in bold on my tombstone after the Queen murdered me with her bare hands, and I'd deserve it. I wanted to hate what Xavier was, but how could I? He was doing his job, and if it wasn't him, someone else would have taken his place, and I probably would never have seen him again.

Was this really better? He controlled a part of me. A primal part I hadn't known existed. It made me want to tear his clothes off whenever I laid eyes on him. I couldn't let it go or control it for that matter.

He also didn't have to tell me about Anne. He could have been an utter arse about it and screwed her, but he'd told me, and it warmed my cold cynical heart. I was sure the Queen would be pissed about the pictures of us out tonight, but if she knew the alternative she'd have agreed with my judgment. I had the perfect way to spin it, a paparazzo in my pocket.

People were on the look out now, and if we gave them something it was better than them hunting until they dug something up, and since I didn't want to be outed, I had to make strategic choices until I was back in my country and married.

The friendship I couldn't explain other than I trusted him. Chances were I would get fucked up the arse, and not in the way I wanted, but I'd never been allowed to be stupid, so I got one right? I walked a tightrope between country and pleasure, and one misstep would bring it all down.

My phone buzzed, and I picked it up to find a text from a number I didn't recognize. I grinned to myself. He'd already taken the bait.

X: Is this a ruse? Are you having me wait out here all night?

I checked my wristwatch. I still had thirty minutes before I had to be down there.

Louis: Look, you do know how to use a phone.

X: You did tell me to wait down here and freeze my ass off.

X: Because whereas that would be funny for you all tucked into your nice warm bed in your posh penthouse, I had a special night planned with my hand.

I had to bite my knuckles to not burst out laughing.

Louis: Maybe I like the thought of you suffering.

X: That I would believe. Kings have to be sadists.

X: My balls will probably fall off before you even make it down here.

Louis: Well, wouldn't that be a shame.

X: If my balls freeze off I'm sending you a bill for the

funeral, and I am not going cheap.

Louis: By all means get the premium flowers, your balls have treated you well.

X: My future suitors will miss out.

I cringed. I didn't like that thought at all. I'd never been a possessive bastard, but I was feeling it now. I assumed it was because there was unfinished business there. I wasn't done with him. Usually after a one night stand I was done by the next morning.

I closed my eyes and my phone vibrated in my hand again.

X: I'd look pretty amusing without balls. Maybe that would distract from my face.

Louis: Would you take to going trouser-less?

X: Clearly.

Louis: Your face is lovely.

X: A face only a prince could endure.

X: Doesn't really have a ring to it.

X: Wait, look, there is proof to take to the tabloids, you like my face. ;)

Louis: You type much too fast to get any sort of reply.

X: Since I shun company I have become quite proficient with my hands.

Louis: Double entendre. Very nice.

X: And here I thought that would at least get me a lol.

X: What? Have you never had text sex? You need quick thumbs so the moment doesn't die.

I felt the statement all the way to my dick.

Louis: No, I haven't had the privilege. Evidence and all.

X: 'tis a right shame. Nothing like a quickie over text or the phone. Some naughty pics mixed in there.

Louis: Yes, that's just what I need, my grandmother seeing my penis all over the place.

X: I'd buy that paper.

I typed out a few messages and subsequently deleted them. He'd already seen it.

Louis: After the other night?

X: For the spank bank.

He added a tiny hand emoji and I couldn't help but laugh.

Louis: Emojis really?

X: Is that beneath your highness?

Louis: I didn't believe grown adults used them.

X: Do the servants who text for you judge you when you use them?

Louis: If servants sent messages for me, you could be assured you wouldn't be on the list.

X: Scared I'll say something?

Louis: Maybe a little.

X: I did sign on your dotted line. I don't think I can even talk about the encounter with you.

What a charming and funny bastard. I didn't want to like him as much as I did.

Louis: Look at you being good.

X: I can be good when there is motivation.

It was getting hot in my hotel room. It would be entirely too easy to let the conversation turn to sex. Sex Xavier had already turned me down for, and I wanted.

X: Oh so slow.

Louis: It takes me time to formulate a response.

X: Is my wit too much for you to handle?

Louis: Hardly.

X: Guarded then?

Louis: As if you have to ask.

X: I'm still a little shocked you put your actual number in my phone.

Louis: Moment of stupidity.

X: Then what would you call asking to be friends?

Louis: Insanity.

X: They do say the years of inbreeding make y'all unstable.

That bastard.

Louis: There has been plenty of genetic diversity in recent years.

X: Can I quote you on that?

X: I'd love to tell the tabloids how many mister-resses the queen has had.

Just imagining the Queen unfaithful was a laugh, and more so her sex life. I gaged.

Louis: I would prefer not to know of my grandmother's sex life.

X: What a shame. I have so much material.

Louis: I picked the wrong friend, didn't I?

X: I tried to tell you.

I laughed in spite of myself again. I found the cynical vibe he put out charming. I was daft. At that moment Anne flounced into the room. She was wearing little more than scraps of clothing, but I really couldn't say much as she'd been photographed in less, much less, well naked, so what did it matter? At least all the naughty bits were covered.

"Do you even have anything on underneath that?" I couldn't help but ask.

"Does tape count?"

I coughed. "Hardly."

"Do you like?" She spun for me.

"Of course. It's lovely, but you do remember who's going to get an earful about this?"

"Which makes it not my problem." Her dark eyes glinted as she said it.

"You're going to need a stack of NDAs."

She giggled and then winked. "Please, this isn't for the boys."

"Who is it for?"

"Me. You really are dense sometimes."

I narrowed my eyes. "I'm not sure I believe you."

"Women dress up for themselves and other women. I could wear a paper bag to the club and if I wanted to fuck, I'd have offers. Dudes are easy."

I shrugged. "Okay, you have a point there."

"Are you ready?"

X: Still freezing. When you get the funeral invitation for my balls you'll know why.

I smiled at my phone as I started to type a reply.

"Who are you texting?" Anne asked. "You never text."

"No one."

She looked at me, and I was positive she didn't believe me, but what could I say? Even if she knew my secret, we both knew it couldn't go anywhere so there was no point.

Louis: Reassure your balls, we'll be down shortly.

X: Are you sure you want me to do this?

I was blown away by his message. It was one thing for him to warn me, but asking if I was sure when I'd offered the pictures. What I'd wanted to believe about him was wrong, and I knew my gut reaction to want to be his friend was right.

Louis: Why wouldn't I be sure?

I wanted to hear it from Xavier. I wanted him to tell me it was a bad idea. I wanted my bad decision validated for once.

X: You know what they are going to print if these pictures get sold.

Louis: I'm sure I know what they'll print. But I also can't keep her in anymore. People our age go out. She's bored, and she'll just start going alone if I don't let her. I've never been able to stop her before.

X: Yeah, I assumed that's what you'd say. Want me to take a few pictures in the club?

Louis: Can you get in?

X: That's where I'm asking for your help.

XAVIER

I had my camera ready when they came down. There was only one other guy with me when I took the pictures which their bodyguards happened to block, while also giving me much better shots from the other side. It was masterful how fluid it was. They were in coats and dark sunglasses despite the hour, like any other pictures of a celebrity going out at night. They were good shots though, and Eran would give me a bonus for them. It was just a start to the assumption he had in his head. He was one of the best in the business, and he was seldom wrong. It was why he was the editor for FMZ, one of the largest gossip shows on television. He also had the money to pay guys like me to suss out his hunches. Thus here I was.

Word would be out quick the royals were going out for the night, so my biggest tip was where they were going. While others were combing the city and trying their contacts to figure out where, I'd be waiting there to take pictures of them walking in, and hopefully Louis could work his magic to get me in the back so I could get some pics of the action. It was a stretch, but it would keep Eran interested in the story and me here, which I wasn't sure Louis knew, but I wasn't about to point out the fact. I'd already told him what they'd print, so my conscience was clear.

As soon as they were in their vehicle, I sprinted to where my bike was sitting and slipped my camera into one of the saddle bags, and I was off. Riding was one of the ways I stayed ahead of the pack. I could park anywhere, be off the thing in a minute, and get in front, or stay behind even the most evasive drivers. A few had adopted my trick, but we were still in the minority among our kind. I would beat them to Seven. I was sure of it.

I had enough time standing out in back of the club to miss smoking again. Instead I played with my camera, adjusting the settings, and testing it so I could get quick shots of them walking into the club. Minutes later I got what I needed and retreated to my bike to send off the photos. They wouldn't beat the guy who'd been there with me when the royals had left the hotel. I bet he sent them as soon as he shot them, but they were better, and I knew where they were.

Once they were uploaded and sent off I packed my equipment back in the saddle bags and sent off a text to Louis.

X: Any chance?

Louis: My body man is waiting at the back for you. You're lucky I find you amusing.

I grinned and pocketed my cell phone camera, there was no way I was getting in with my DSLR. Clubs didn't keep celebrities coming back by allowing my kind inside. They had their own promo photogs anyway, so it would have to look like an innocent cell phone photo, which I could make good enough to print. It was all about the know-how.

I walked up to the back to find the giant brute from the first night waiting there for me. He grunted as I thanked him for waving me in, and it was off to the VIP area. Again, it would look strange if I was in there, but I couldn't get enough of Louis, and from what I'd heard of Anne, she wasn't one to stay in lounges. She liked to be out with the people. A detail which pissed off the Gotha house more than anything.

I didn't book it. I took my time getting a drink, letting them settle in. Word would start to get out where they were as soon as Eran broke the story online. People would show up. The club would get packed, and I had to work my timing. I wanted intoxicated, but not to overstay my welcome. So I had a drink and let them settle in, and get comfortable. If I'd been in their face from the start, they'd be on edge and uncomfortable. I was sure Louis had told Anne I'd be here, but alcohol did a lot to reducing the give a fuck.

The crowd was starting to thicken, and I knew it was my time to make my move. Anne had to be feeling itchy in the lounge by now. So I made my way over, half dancing, phone in my pocket. I loathed dancing. And by loathed, I mean it was the worst thing in the known universe, and blending in wasn't my strong suit. I was pretty sure I looked like a stiff robot, and not in the cool robot way. I made bad white guy moves look bad. But if I could wait out in the cold for hours on end for a shot, what was a little fake dancing? The things I did for the love of money.

I scanned the VIP area as I walked around the perimeter. If they were anything like other famous people, they'd be tucked in the back where it was safe from the herds. Most photos I took inside clubs were celebrities canoodling in the back with new significant others. They were grainy and dark and mostly hard to tell it was actually the people we were claiming they were. It was their way of living their perfect lives on the wild side. If they were front and center it was usually a ruse, and they wanted pictures splashed all over the tabloids because they were short on work or promoting something. I took those as well. I enjoyed money.

But Louis wasn't in the back. They had a booth with a great view from between two pillars. No hats, which I'd known, but still, this had to all be for me. It made me have feelings. I didn't like feelings.

What was Louis playing at? This was a favor repaid but in spades. It was too much. He couldn't be that nice. No one was that nice. Maybe he wanted something from me, and I just wasn't seeing it. I needed to keep my guard up. I wasn't about to cover something up for them. Or so I told myself.

The royals weren't the only ones in the club tonight. There was a Canadian singer who I found entirely overrated, but that didn't stop me from getting a picture of him as he tried to chat up Anne. It was laughable. She was way too hot for him. I couldn't image the two of them dating, but they both had long histories of stupid public stunts. I kept that in the back of my brain to watch for.

My gaze landed on Louis and a man. He was chatting lazily enough, but there was more. I wanted to get closer. The guy leaned in and picked something off his lapel. Was it an ex? Or maybe a new prospect. I'd signed an NDA, but could I print this? My stomach knotted. I didn't want to be that guy. It was hard enough to be gay, and outing a celebrity before they were ready was just not my thing. I had rules. So I wouldn't take the picture, but there was more to it. I didn't like the way he was looking at Louis. Or maybe it was the familiarity. They were all smiles, and by the color in Louis' cheeks I could tell he was well on his way to being intoxicated.

I didn't really know Louis. He'd claimed it had been awhile, that I was the first in a while, but maybe it was what he said to everyone. Maybe he was feeding this guy the same lines he'd fed me. I was imagining him telling the guy he was lovely, and it made me sick.

I couldn't stop watching, and I'd almost missed Anne leaving the lounge. I had to tear myself away. I had to do my job. This was an opportunity, a favor, and he could sleep with whomever he wanted. We weren't anything. I'd been the one who turned down sleeping with him again. It wasn't my business, after all. So instead of torturing myself by watching the encounter, I went to follow Anne.

LOUIS

He'd texted me an hour ago, and I still hadn't seen him. I didn't expect him to make it into the VIP lounge, but come on. I expected to find him watching Anne and I at some point, but he was nowhere to be seen. He was either that good or had been distracted by a piece of ass. Or he had what he needed. I didn't know, but I was seething about it for no reason at all.

"Louis?"

I looked up to find Drake Chad, an old friend from Eton. He was to inherit a dukedom, and thus we'd spent a lot of time in the same circles growing up.

"What are you doing here?"

"What, I can't be vacationing in Canada?"

I laughed, raising my brows in mock questioning. "I thought nude beaches on tropical islands were more your style."

"Heard about that, did you?" he asked, no blush in his cheeks. In fact he was smirking, like the smug bastard he was.

He could pull it off too. Tall, blond, and abs that went on for miles on his lanky body. I'd never made that mistake though, and he'd tried.

"I heard you had a lot of local dick in your mouth too."

"You'd be doing the same if you were me."

"I almost wish I were." And it was true. I didn't think he was out to his parents yet, but coming out wasn't about to affect his inheritance, unless his parents decided to be real tools. And as products of the seventies, I doubted they would be. Not like it was such a big deal anymore to most. He didn't have parliament to contend with. My uncle couldn't even get remarried without the Queen's approval, and he was pushing sixty.

"You don't. You've got it pretty good."

I gave him a flat look. "I'm here on state business. What are you here for? Chasing arse?"

"Hardly, I'm here with the RAF."

I wanted to laugh because that was as much of a joke as him taking a gap year to find himself on a tropical island. "You? In the Royal Air Force?"

"Yeah, we're just training and such. We came over with you."

"Why didn't you tell me?"

He lifted a shoulder. "I figured we'd talk once you were here."

And here I'd been for two weeks and this was the first I was seeing of him. "Here we are." I offered him a fake smile.

"Yes, we are." He looked around. "I'm sure you're in some swanky place while we're held up in a barracks. See, posh."

"Like the officer quarters aren't nice." I rolled my eyes,

glancing around. I tried to keep it nonchalant because I didn't want him asking questions. We were old friends after all, but I felt like I was being watched, and I wanted to know if it was Xavier at last. I didn't see anyone, and I cursed to myself.

"Looking for someone?" he asked, stepping closer.

"Just at the crowds," I lied as I brought my drink to my lips.

He looked me over sitting there and dragged his tongue over his teeth. "Since we are both here on official business…" He titled his head and took a drag of his own drink.

Interesting. "What are you saying?" I asked, already knowing his answer and mine, but it was my job to be two steps ahead, and I didn't want him to know I had any idea what he was talking about.

"I think you know what I'm saying. We could help each other out for awhile, or longer, considering your position."

And there it was, not as subtle as I thought. Bravo for the balls. I sat back and crossed my ankle over knee and looked him over. He was attractive, but I'd never been interested. I should want his offer. It would have been so easy to have a mistress so to say, but I couldn't bring myself to actually do it. My moral code forbade it.

"Hmmm…" I said, because he was clearly waiting for an instant yes.

He acted as if he was using the table to lean on, but in the meantime got closer and whispered. "We could give it a trial run tonight. Give it a go and see if—" The smug look was back. "We're compatible." His voice was all sex, and whereas I was sure this whole act worked on anyone else, I found it a big production.

"Not tonight. I promised Anne a night out."

He looked around. "I don't see her."

Now I was sure we were being watched, and if it was anyone but Xavier—well it wouldn't look great to anyone. I glanced around again. "Why me?" I asked him. I was clearly going to have to use stronger measures to talk him out of this, but not to the point where he thought I was spurning him. I didn't want to put a bad taste in his mouth as he clearly knew what I was.

"Because I've always been attracted to you, and for a long time I thought you were out of my league, but I started to think about it and well, you're screwed. You'll never come out, and you're going to have to marry eventually, so why not have some place to get what you need? It benefits us both."

"And how do you see it benefiting you?" I asked, my mind working overtime to figure out how to get out of this.

"Because I want my cock in your arse."

It took a lot to keep my face neutral. There was no way I was ever going to let him put his cock in my arse. If I'd even wanted to consider it, he was bending over, but no. Not a chance. Instead of giving him the look I wanted, I went with smug and unobtainable. I was good at putting out that vibe, years of practice.

"How long-term could that last? I'm sure you're going to want to settle down eventually."

He lifted his shoulders. "Maybe, but I'd rather sleep around, and since you'd be married, I'm sure that wouldn't be an issue. I could have my relationship cake, so to speak, and eat out too."

I nearly spit my beer. "Crude."

He winked, and I was really starting to wonder how we were such good mates as kids.

"I don't think it's a good idea while we're on duty."

He acted like it was not a big deal. "Think about it, and if you change your mind, you know where to find me."

"Sure."

He shook my hand and got out of my hair, and I'd never been more grateful. Now where the hell was Xavier, and Anne for that matter? She was gone like Drake had pointed out. She must have left as soon as he'd walked up. She'd never been a big fan of him. I wanted to go in search of her, but I also didn't want to leave the safety of the lounge. Not with the rumours I was looking for a wife floating around. It was deal with flocks of women or possibly not see Anne or Xavier for the rest of the night. I considered it, and then was on my feet. I needed to satisfy my curiosity and figure out where Xavier was.

XAVIER

Anne was exquisite. She was thin, too thin for my taste. She always had been because of the drugs I assumed, but she looked better than she did in recent years. If Eran thought she was still on drugs, he was wrong. He was probably just chasing another story because she looked more alive than I'd ever seen her look, not that I had more than pictures to go on. But she was more filled out, and she wasn't ashen. There was a nice flush to her skin as she danced, and the surrounding patrons took notice. Men and women were trying to get her attention by dancing with her, but she did a good job of keeping to herself. She'd dance and move on. The lovely black and crystal dress moved like it was painted on. She knew how to dress her body. If I hadn't met her brother first, I might had gone after her. Her energy was truly something.

I snapped a few pictures after I realized I'd been standing watching her for longer than I should be. I hoped no one else would take too many photos or get creepy. She deserved to be free like this. The thought of being the center of attention made my skin crawl. I'd made a fair amount of mistakes in my life, and none of them where documented. She wasn't allowed to put a toe out of line without it being a state issue. I couldn't imagine being a recovering addict in that light. If there was enough reason for a relapse, that was it. At least she had more wiggle room than Louis. Younger siblings were almost expected to be the ones who acted out.

I slipped through the crowd and back to the bar. There was no reason for me to stay. I should be tempted to stick around and look for some fun, but I couldn't bring myself to. I kept seeing Louis with that douche, and the way he touched Louis made me want to slug him. I'd already had him pegged as a tool, he was seeping fucksicle from his pores. I didn't like people in general, but the guy made me slightly homicidal. I was better off seeing this side of Louis before I allowed myself to get too wrapped up in this friendship.

I ordered and then turned back to find Anne on the floor. She was still there going strong. I should send these photos before anyone whipped out their cell phone and beat me to it. I could cash in and leave, but I already knew Eran would want more. He'd ask me to extend. Follow them for the rest of the tour and see what I could get, but I couldn't. I wanted to go back to my bubble where I didn't have to deal with people.

A hand slid over my shoulder, and hot breath against my ear. "She keeping your attention?"

"You did invite me here so I could do my job."

"And here I thought I'd at least be part of your focus." He stepped around and took the stool in front of me. "You look hungry when you look at her."

"I can admire a lovely form."

"I'm envious of your choice."

"It's always been about personality for me." I turned around to face him. "Do you really want there to be pictures of us?"

"I can't talk to a guy at a bar?"

I raised a brow.

He ordered a gin and tonic. "Then it's like we are both just sitting here."

"I'm starting to think you get off on this cloak and dagger shit."

He side-eyed me as he laid a twenty on the bar top. "Maybe. So your job only involves Anne?"

"Are you disappointed to not be the center of attention for once?" I wasn't even sure why I was being hostile or what my issue was.

He rose a brow but didn't look over at me. His drink was placed in front of him, and he played with the glass. "I would have thought the other night would have made that evident, or possibly our friendship."

"Your attention seemed to be otherwise engaged." I looked over at him.

He turned to look at me. "You can't be serious."

"It's none of my business."

He scrubbed a hand over his face. "He's an old school mate."

"Again, that's your business."

"I've never touched him."

I looked back at the bar because I really didn't want to be the subject of any rumors. "I never said you did."

"Then what are you saying?"

Why was he pushing this? I didn't care. I couldn't care. "I'm not saying a single thing. You were the one who asked why I wasn't over there."

"Yes, and you haven't answered."

"I thought you two needed your privacy."

He scoffed. "Hardly."

"Do you want pictures published of him picking lint off your shirt?" I snuck another glance to gage his reaction. I realized how stupid I was. This guy was nothing to me. Maybe a friend, and I'd not taken a photo, which was mostly harmless but could have netted me a lot of green all because what? It wasn't like he had a dick in his mouth. I wasn't outing him. There would be speculation at most. But I knew the truth, and I couldn't do it.

"He propositioned me." He brought his drink to his lips. "I don't know why I'm telling you this."

"Of course he did." Everyone probably did. He was the prince after all. As I suspected the 'no one knows he's gay' thing was probably a line he used. It was probably the worst kept secret in Britain. "But again, no need to explain."

His damn hand was on my arm again. "But I want to explain. Why are you so hostile?"

"I'm not. We had a thing. It's over. Sleep with whomever you want."

"I have no desire to sleep with him. But you told me you didn't want to sleep with me anymore. So why are you so angry?"

"Then how does he know?" I hissed under my breath. "How would he possibly know you're gay if it's really this thing you never tell anyone? Or maybe plenty know, and it's just a line you feed to guys to get them into bed. Get them to sign your little NDA to keep your secret out of the press." Why was I doing this? I wasn't even drunk, so why couldn't I shut my damn mouth? "You want to know why I'm hostile? Because you claim to want to be friends, and then lie to me right off the bat. I don't like being lied to. So you can take your lies and shove them. I don't have time for a fake friendship."

He was struck dumb. He just sat there and blinked at me. If I dared I would have taken a picture of it. The look was entirely against his personality, and I rather liked seeing it. I bet no one had ever stood up to him like this his entire life.

"We were school mates as I said, and he was gay, so I talked to him about it when I started to realise, but even now I see it was a mistake, as he wants something from me."

He caught me off guard.

"You assume the worst of me, and you barely know me." He turned back to his drink and finished it in one pull and then signaled to the bartender to bring him another round.

"You seemed overly familiar with him, and what was I to expect? It's hard to believe a prince doesn't sleep around."

"I'd love to sleep around, and I probably would be that person if I were straight, but I don't have the luxury. I keep up the image the tabloids print as a cover." He pressed his eyes closed, and I could see real pain there. "I didn't sleep with you under false pretenses. I don't have to make up lies to get arse."

I ground my teeth. There was that thing. I didn't want to like him and here he was making a lot of sense. "When you put it that way."

He nodded but still wouldn't look at me. "What did he

want from you?"

He took a sip of the fresh gin and tonic. "He wants to be my mistress."

I coughed. "Wow, bold move."

He forced a smile. "He wants to be able to say he put his dick in the King's arse." He downed his second drink, and I was starting to be concerned he was going to become intoxicated in public and draw more attention than his sister. "Which would make him more of a liability than anything worthwhile, not that I wanted him to start with."

"This probably isn't the best place to have this conversation." I looked around, thankful no one seemed to have noticed the prince was out here.

"I'm sure he'd write a book at some point. Or maybe he actually enjoys the idea of the prestige or even he's attracted to me, but it's too hard to think there isn't some motive there. He even admitted he'd enjoy it because he'd be able to sleep around."

The hits just kept on coming. No wonder he was so down. I felt even more like an ass. "He said that to your face?"

Louis nodded and told the bartender to keep them coming. He started to ask if he knew Louis, and he waved him off. "He did. Nothing like charming me into bed with the fact that while I'm doing my duty and marrying a woman to produce heirs he can fuck whatever piece of arse he wants."

"We need to get you back to your hotel."

"Why don't you take some pictures first?"

I growled through gritted teeth and grabbed ahold of his arm a bit too harshly. "I'm trying to be the friend you want me to be, and we are getting your ass out of here before you cause a scene."

"You should use it. Probably the only reason you accepted my pathetic request to be friends." He picked up the third drink and went to make quick work on it while the bartender was still asking him why he looked so familiar.

I got to my feet and went to grab Anne. Where the hell was Doug or whatever his name was?

"Bailing on me, huh?" Louis called after.

Anne was in the middle of a group of thirsty guys, and I couldn't get to her. It was back to the lounge area. Where I found Doug watching.

"I need you."

He grunted at me.

"I'm not doing this for fun."

He titled his head.

"He's wasted, and I know this isn't your job but he's going to make a scene. Get Anne."

His brows knit together, and he took a closer look at Louis and sighed. "What did you do?"

"Wasn't me. I'm the one trying to make sure there aren't pictures."

I turned, figuring he'd come himself and went back to Louis' side.

"Doug thinks it's time for you to go."

He scoffed. "Naw, I'm having a nice chat with this bloke." He half pointed at the bartender.

"Is he the prince?" he asked. "I heard he's in town or sumpin."

I laughed. "He gets that all the time. Dead ringer isn't he?"

The guy looked deflated. "Right, if it were him he'd be

staying in the lounge."

People were starting to look and whisper though. He needed to get out of here now. I swear if there was one picture printed of me next to the prince I would commit a murder. Thankfully, Doug showed up at that point and Anne was at his side. She looked to me for an explanation.

"I don't know." I held up my hands. What did they want from me?

They encouraged him to get to his feet, and I slipped back into the crowd. There were too many people paying attention, and it felt like the room was closing in. Blackness started to eat away at my vision, and I couldn't control my breathing. I did what I could and all I knew was I had to get out of there before I lost it.

LOUIS

Louis: Thank you.

X: It was nothing.

But it wasn't nothing. It was possibly the nicest thing anyone had ever done for me. I was still waiting for the pictures to start showing up. I'd checked first thing this morning, and nothing, which scared me more. Someone had to have recognized me. I wanted to ask him, but it took me twenty minutes to decide if it was abusing our friendship.

Louis: I'm shocked there aren't any pictures of me being carried out of there.

X: I think you got drunk so fast and had your back to most of the club so no one except the bartender recognized you.

Shit.

Louis: So he did.

X: I threw him off the trail. Said you get that all the time. Can't say it will save you since they are printing the pictures of you and Anne, but who knows if he'll figure out he has a story and actually goes to someone.

I wanted to bang my head. But at least there weren't pictures of Doug practically carrying me out of there.

Louis: Maybe he won't.

X: There are still some nice guys left out there.

And he was one of them whether he saw it or not. I thought about it more, and I hadn't done enough. I felt like I was in his debt. I wasn't sure how I felt about that.

Louis: How can I repay you?

He was typing for a long time, which drove me a little mad. I wished I had some place to be, but Doug had the social secretary cancel my morning after carrying me out of there. So I have to stay in and claim I have a mild cold.

I couldn't take it anymore. "Doug? Can you do me a favour?"

Doug wasn't happy about the favour, but he went to find Xavier, and I paced until they returned.

"I thought we agreed this was a bad idea?" Xavier slipped into my room behind Doug.

Doug looked at me and shook his head. "I'll be in my room."

"Really twisting his arm, aren't you?"

I looked between the door Doug vanished behind and back to Xavier. "He doesn't want to like you, but he does after last night. Be sure of that."

His brows rose. "You're sure? You didn't find his grunting cold? It comes off cold to me."

"I've known him many years. Believe me, he hates the fact that he likes you."

"I'll try and read into his grunts better next time." Xavier looked around. "Swanky place you have here."

"It's nice…" I didn't want to talk about the hotel suite.

"Nice?" He spun around. "I guess it has nothing on the palace." He said with an air of disdain.

"I don't pick where we stay." I took a seat in one of the chairs and gestured towards the other. "Tea?"

He stayed there in the entryway like he was scared to come in further. "I'm good." He did this little shuffle of his feet, looking down, as he slid his hands in his pockets. He felt out of place. It was one thing when he barely knew me and I led him into a suite in his city, but here, in the daylight without alcohol, he felt like he didn't belong.

"I don't feel like I belong either."

"Huh?" He looked up.

"You're thinking you don't fit in."

He tilted his head. "Does anyone?"

I poured the tea into the china, forcing myself not to look back at him. "There are days I do, but most of the time I'm terrified of the day my Grandmother dies."

He came around the back of my chair and sat in the one beside me.

"Decided to stay?"

"I'd probably have left if you'd have said anything else."

I nearly spilled the scalding tea when my head jerked up. "You take pleasure in the fact that I don't fit into my life?"

"No, I think only a narcissist would believe he fit in here and deserved it. Used to it would make more sense."

"I'm not even used to it."

I poured him a cup and offered it to him, and he proceeded to add entirely too much sugar. I doctored mine with a little milk and sat back.

"You don't have to do this." He took a sip of his tea before setting it aside and returning to his previous fidgeting.

"Do what?" I was curious what he believed this to be.

"This." He gestured between us. "Friendship because you feel indebted to me."

"I guess I do feel indebted, but I would continue to repay you in picture currency if I felt so inclined."

"Then why am I up here?"

I didn't have an answer. Not a good one.

"You ask about repaying me and then invite me up. It's pretty evident."

I gave him a flat look. "You take too long to reply."

"Because I don't want anything, and I was trying to come up with a nice way to let you down."

"Excuse me?" I asked.

"I didn't want to hurt your ego when you offered to repay me in sexual favors."

I scoffed and nearly spit my tea at him. I dabbed my lips with a napkin and laughed.

"Let's see, you offer to repay me and then invite me up." He smirked.

"I wasn't looking for a repeat of the other night."

He crossed his arms over his chest. "Then what were you looking for princeling?"

"Princeling?"

"You heard me."

I took another measured sip of my tea, making him wait for my response. "I was considering pictures of a stunt to repay you, not sexual favours." Truly, I hadn't thought that far when

I'd told Doug to go get him.

He leaned forward, resting his forearms on his knees. "Too bad. Sexual favors sound more fun." He got up and stretched. "I'll go back to my post."

"You just going to sit out there all day?"

"I've done worse." He turned to leave.

I forced myself to stay sitting. To not get up and follow him. To not pin him to the damn wall and repay him in sexual favours.

LOUIS

Finding excuses to go down to him became my new mission. While kissing babies and showing my smiling face around the province, my mind was always working. I had this obsession with being around him.

"Again?" he asked as I took a seat in my now usual place.

"Do you ever go home?"

"I don't spend all day here," he said simply without offering me more of an explanation.

"You just sit around and wait for us to go to dinner?"

"And the few nights you've been out elsewhere."

I rubbed a hand over the back of my head. "You know you could probably wait inside."

"Or where you're going to dinner. Also not a huge secret."

"I've noticed. And yet you're the only one who waits here."

"I'm throwing you a bone."

This caught me off guard. "Is that so?"

"You have made a habit of coming down here. How else would we get this time?"

"It's also benefiting you."

"Sure, okay." He flashed me a smile.

"Do you want me to stop?"

"No, it's not terrible."

I scoffed and refrained from crossing my arms over my chest.

"How very princely of you to throw a tantrum when you don't hear what you want."

I glared over at him and his grin widened.

"You enjoy teasing me?"

"How could I not? I bet it doesn't happen often."

"You'd be correct in your assumption."

His eyes lit up, drawing me in. I wanted to scoot closer. Act the way I did at Eton before I knew how my actions could be interpreted. Act on pure instinct, instead of the rules adulthood had so firmly planted in my psyche.

"We should be smoking or something. I don't know how you deal with all this sitting around."

"Because I like my own company. I don't need to have every minute of every day scheduled." He had me there.

"And what do you do with your own company?"

"I create stories in my mind, sometimes I draw them, but I can spend hours creating things."

"What kinds of things?"

He looked at me for a long moment. Maybe he was deciding if I was worthy. He must have decided something because he flipped open the flap on his messenger bag and rummaged around inside. He must have had a load of stuff in there because it took him a bit to find what he was after and when he did he withdrew a notebook.

"They aren't very good." But he flipped open the book, holding it so I couldn't see. I didn't try and get a glimpse, instead waiting for him to come to me. "I don't really share them, but since I have enough of your secrets now I figure you won't really tell anyone."

I rolled my eyes at him and held out my hand for the book. He didn't place it in my grasp right away, but I was a patient man and at last he did. I watched him until his fingers released it, and then dropped my gaze to see what he'd opened the book to. It was me, and yet, not me. It was my likeness but transformed into an elf. My ears were elongated and my hair longer still. The important parts were there, and he had this uncanny way of doing the eyes. They were lifelike and drew me into the piece. It was all sketched in black and white.

"It's lovely."

"You would think so since that one bares a close resemblance to you."

"You're the one who drew it," I pointed out.

"Mistaken judgment."

I started to flip the page, but he was too fast and grabbed the book back.

"What's on the next page."

"You don't want to see."

"Of course I do. As I said, you are quite talented, and they are lovely."

"I thought I was lovely." He smiled at me, tucking the book back in in bag.

My lips curled up at the ends. This was a game, and I

wanted more of his work. "You know you are, but I want the next page."

"What are you going to give me for it?" He sat back and eyed me.

"Hmmm." I tapped my chin.

"A picture of me."

His brows rose. "What kind of picture?"

I wanted to say anything, but it was such a dangerous word. "It depends on what your intended usage is."

"If it's just for me?"

The words formed on my tongue before I could stop them. "Then you can have whatever you want."

Both his brows rose halfway up his forehead. "You must really trust me."

"I do," I said realising I did.

"And if it's to publish?" he asked, and I was grateful he changed the subject.

"We can talk about it, but you have to decide and then let me have the book." If I was going to give away that much I wanted to make sure I didn't just get a single picture.

He held out his hand. "Deal."

I took it and shook. "Now which is it?"

"I want the one for my personal usage."

I felt his words all the way to my groin, and it would have been pretty evident how I felt about it had I been asked to stand at that moment. Thankfully I didn't have to get up.

Xavier reached into his bag and pulled the book back out. "Don't let it go to your head."

I took it and looked at him without opening it. "Do I appear in more of them?"

"I tend to focus on a muse for a time before moving on." He shrugged it off like it was nothing.

I liked this idea too much and not at all. I didn't want to know about previous muses. And I didn't want to come face to face with them inside. Maybe he was a little right about how I was used to being the centre of attention, but it never mattered to me before him. I wanted to be the centre of his attention.

"Aren't you going to look?" He gestured at the book.

"How many other dudes am I going to find in here?"

"Who said I only draw men?"

I nodded. "Right, I assumed—how many other muses am I going to find in here?"

"Look at the book or give it back." He held out his hand for it.

I flipped it open, and he sat back and watched me. It was stunning, and I quickly forgot I was looking for other muses. It was a story of sorts, and I was a reoccurring character. It could have been a graphic novel. It was quite extensive and extremely well done.

"Spectacular. You are incredibly talented." I didn't want to put it down. I wanted to sneak off with it and indulge in reading it.

He half smiled. "At least you asked for the tame one."

I coughed and looked over at him. "Excuse me?"

"You heard me."

"There is another?" I asked.

He pulled a second from his back without looking down. "You think I only have one sketch book?" He grinned at me. "So when are we talking photos?"

"You can come up and do it now." I was hoping to get a glimpse of the other book.

"You're just trying to get me into bed." He stood and brushed off his pants.

"I don't have to try." I got to my feet and offered him back the book since it was only a third of the way filled and I'd been through it all.

"What do you mean?" he asked.

"If I wanted you back in bed I'd have you back in my bed."

"You're too smug."

"But right. I already know how I'd do it."

"How?"

I smiled ruefully and walked back inside.

XAVIER

He was a smug bastard, and clearly I had some issues I needed to talk out because that shit turned me on. I almost followed him inside, but that's what he wanted. The part of me that was defiant barely won out over the part of me that was raging hard. If he was so sure about being able to get me, he could show me. The ball was in his court. And to prove my point I took the night off. It was the only way I could to get to him.

"Eran, what else do you have for me? I'm bored. Who else is here?"

"Have you not been paying attention?"

"No. I've been stalking the royals for you."

"True true. Give me a sec." I heard him typing. "When you head to Vancouver tomorrow there will be a lot more going on."

I'd almost forgotten the tour was moving on and I'd be going home. I wasn't sure how it made me feel. I'd almost gotten attached to the hotel and the area. "You want me to stay?"

"I wouldn't mind you working double time if you're up for it."

"I'll never say no to extra money." Which wasn't entirely true. I could have cashed in on Louis but I hadn't. But I would never tell anyone who paid for my work that because they'd black ball me.

"Does this mean you'll finally take a staff position?"

"No," I groaned, switching hands with the phone. "You know I like variety."

"Yeah, it's how you get rich, but not what pays the bills."

I clenched my teeth. "It's paid the bills just fine."

"It's getting harder to get shots, you and I both know it. There are more and more freelancers, and celebrities are getting more private. I could set you up in LA. The relocation fee alone, we could put your mug on TV here and there. Then when you get too old to hoof it around chasing after these people you could get a producer gig. I know you know this."

My throat constricted, and my lungs refused oxygen. Even him mentioning the idea of putting me on TV. I couldn't. My stomach turned and tried to expel what I'd eaten. "I can't right now." It was hard to force the words out.

"The job might not be there in a year. You should really take me up on this soon."

"I know I know," I said, knowing it was impossible.

"I'll send you a list of my wants for Vancouver." He knew when to stop pushing. The job was good. Who wouldn't want to work for FMZ? It was the cream of the crop so to speak.

"Perfect."

"But don't neglect the royals for any of this crap. There are lots of drugs moving in and out of Vancouver."

"Roger that." Who didn't go to British Columbia without smoking a little weed? I laughed to myself.

He hung up the phone, and I was left alone in my room in a strange city with not a thing to do. I could have gone back and waited for the prince's usual dinner outing, but I didn't have it in me. I was starting to get attached, and I was starting to feel like his toy.

I wondered if he'd miss me. So I ordered pizza and played chicken to see if he'd text me first.

LOUIS

He. Wasn't. Fucking. There.

The first and only constant in my life, which is a little sad if you ask me, had skipped out. I liked knowing what to expect. I liked when things were expected. My life was enough chaos and stress. So when I expected something, I wanted it there. He wasn't waiting for me when we left for dinner. He wasn't at the restaurant and he wasn't there when we got back. We were getting boring. The paparazzi had stopped caring.

What if he'd gone back to Chicago? I had his number and could easily get his address, which sounded super creepy in my mind, but what good would anything do if he decided he was done? A shot of me showing up at his place wouldn't be so great for my closeted self.

I didn't think I could let it go like this.

My mind spun as I paced my hotel room. It was a good thing we were getting a change of scenery tomorrow. I was going stir crazy after this amount of time. Sure we'd been all over the territory, but there wasn't that much up here in the frozen tundra of the world. British Columbia had a lot more to offer, and I was rather looking forward to kicking back and enjoying that part of the tour.

A pang hit the center of my chest. My mind kept going back to Xavier. He could have decided there was nothing here, since he knew Anne and I wouldn't do anything risky with him watching. Maybe he took another job. It was his right. There was nothing holding him here, but I had hoped and I'd been trying to lure him back in.

I needed to get pissed and forget this foolishness. What was I even thinking? I picked up my phone and then set it back down. I didn't want to come off desperate. I'd leave it alone and see if he showed up tomorrow for our grand exit. And by grand exit, I meant getting on a plane and doing a lot of waving.

There was a knock on my door. One I wasn't expecting. A tiny flash of hope filled me before rationality squashed it. It wasn't possible for him to get through my security. The second emotion to hit me was panic. What if it was Drake coming to seek me out again? Since he was an old friend and part of the RAF he'd get waved through. I didn't want to answer the door.

Maybe I'd climb in bed and ignore it.

"Open the door you prat."

Well it clearly wasn't Drake.

"I'm coming."

Anne stood outside the door with a bottle of gin in each hand.

I waved her in. "Maybe I do like you."

She flashed me a grin. "I know."

"You don't have plans tonight?"

She'd been good about staying and having people in for the most part, and I'd avoided it.

"I have plans. I'm here with gin."

I raised a brow in silent questioning.

"Okay, I canceled them. I saw your face when we got back." She grimaced and then got two glasses and filled them with ice at the bar before pouring the gin and adding a splash of tonic. I gratefully took the glass and drank it down.

She stopped mid-sitting and went to get the bottle and soda. "Let's just keep this here."

"Good idea," I said holding it out for a refill.

She obliged me, and then sat back and put her feet on the coffee table. There was something going on with her, and I couldn't quite put my finger on it. Like she was covering something up, but there were none of the normal signs.

"Is there something going on with you?" I asked, feeling like an arse for not asking sooner. I was too wrapped up in my own shit.

She looked at her drink and tucked her hair behind her ear. "Yeah, it's just—" She let out a breath. "I want my image to change, because I know how Gran feels about it, but I also want to have fun, but having fun will create rumors, so I'm trying to ride a fine line. It's hard."

I nodded along with her words. "I can't imagine."

She looked at me with an odd kind of smile. Sympathy maybe? I couldn't read it.

"Yes, you can. You've been walking the line a lot longer and doing a better job of it." She clutched her glass between both hands and pulled her knees in. "So much so no one has even realised. I didn't even know until Drake told me."

I choked on my drink. "What?"

She frowned. "He didn't know I didn't know. Don't blame him."

"Of course I blame him. I talked to him in confidence."

She shook her head. "He was asking how you were and was worried about you. It's hard doing what you're doing."

"What do you mean?" She looked so upset. I forgot about my own stupid issues.

"Being something you're not. I've seen the papers as much as Drake has."

I scoffed and looked at the ceiling. "I can assure you, his concern was nothing more than fishing. He wants to be my mistress." The words tasted vile coming from my lips.

She giggled. "Are you serious?"

"Why does everyone find this funny?"

She shrugged and shook her head. "I don't even know. How strange of him. He needs to back off if it was all fake." She chewed on her lip. "What's going on with you and the paparazzi guy?"

I focused on downing another drink.

"Louis?"

"I like him, and it doesn't matter. I tried to sleep with him again, he turned me down, and then I tried again, and he turned me down again, and, well, frankly it's pathetic."

"How are you doing it?"

"What do you mean?"

"I mean are you making it all about the sex?"

I looked at her funny. I had no idea what she was getting at. "Isn't that what hook ups are about?"

"Well maybe you need to romance him a little. I don't know how stuff with dicks works, but he's a human and humans like romance. Even if people with penises are all sex crazed."

I didn't have words. Maybe it was about more. "Huh."

"You said you liked him. If you want to do more than have sex, tell him. Use your big boy words."

I scowled at her. "I don't think I can let it be more than sex. It has to end when we go home."

She didn't look at me for a few moments. "Why can't you let it be this amazing thing? More than sex with an end date? It's okay to cherish something and know what it is. Like a summer romance. In Canada in the winter. Less romantic but still a thing."

I chuckled. "Maybe."

"It's okay to admit you're a dense prat and I'm right."

I flipped her the bird.

I paced my room late into the night. There was gin involved, and it was a good thing I'd handed my phone over to Doug and made him promise not to give it back to me until the next morning, otherwise I would have given Xavier a lot of power over me with ridiculous drunk text messages.

When I'd had enough that standing wasn't a good idea anymore, I sank into a seat in front of the fire. I stared into the flames and visions of my life danced before my eyes. This was all I had. This was all I would ever have. I had this tiny bit of a romance, and then it would all vanish when I had to replace it with duty. And I would do it. I'd do it for my country, and for my sister, but most of all I'd do it for my grandmother who had spent almost a century upholding our name and title with the utmost dignity. She deserved this. She'd raised my sister and I after our parents died, as normally as could be, all while ruling a country, and she'd already dealt with more than any person should have to bear. Losing her son first and then my sister's addiction. I couldn't be the one to add to it. I couldn't let her down.

"Doug."

"No fucking way."

"I don't give a shit what I said, give me my damn phone back."

"I'm not goin ta do it, Sir."

I held out my hand.

"This isn't a good idea. You made me promise."

I groaned. I had, but this was different. I'd had a damn epiphany. "I will fight you."

"Okay." He sniggered. "Come at me."

I held up my fists and swayed.

"I didn't think so."

"I order you to give me my phone back."

He sighed and got up to cross the room. "Not a good idea, and I will not be held responsible."

"You can go to bed. You did your best."

He put the phone in my hand and shook his head. "G'night." And he left. As simple as that. I didn't blame him. He was stuck between a rock and a hard place with his own duty. I wouldn't get fired keeping someone's phone from them. Although I'd never do that to him, I could see it from his point of view.

Instead of dwelling on what Doug was going to say to my hungover ass tomorrow, it was time to formulate a text. I'd decided to send one, but now I wasn't sure what to say. My brain was too muddled with liquor and it wasn't so easy to think as straight as I needed to. I laid my head back against the sofa. There were more images in the flames. Ones that were going to haunt me for a long time, but maybe I needed to see them.

I lifted my phone to my blurry vision and willed my fingers to work as I opened my messages to Xavier.

Louis: Decided we were too boring?

I didn't want to lay it on too thick. I had a cocky reputation to uphold, and I was pretty sure he thoroughly enjoyed it based on his previous hard ons in my presence. I kept checking the message to see if ellipsis would appear. The bloody bastard had read receipts off so I couldn't tell if he'd even looked at the message.

I passed out that way and was awoken by something poking me.

My head was pounding. The room lurched and bile burned my throat. I peeled one eye open against my body's protest, seeing it was Doug's foot poking my ribs.

"What the hell?"

"Time to wake up." I could hear the smirk in his voice.

"I don't want to." I forced the other eye open to see the sun just barely casting its light over the city. "I hate you and everything you stand for," I grumbled as I swayed on my feet.

"I stand for you and your country."

"I hate it all." I squinted at the time. "Why are we awake?"

"Didn't you say to wake you at six?"

I fell back into a seat on the sofa. "We don't leave until

noon."

"My bad." He shrugged and turned on the frother to steam himself some milk, like the arrogant cockwaffle he was.

"I hate morning people."

"Only when you've had too much to drink." He sniffed his coffee. "Now do you want a coffee?"

"Maybe in three hours." I staggered to the bed and passed back out.

XAVIER

I had a flight to catch, and I wasn't sure how to reply.

I thought about the text as I packed.

I thought about the text as I drove the rented bike to the airport.

I thought about the text as I waited in security.

And as I boarded the plane I still hadn't replied.

Maybe it would be best if I saw him.

Xavier: Where are you staying?

I shoved my phone in my pocket and took a seat, not expecting a reply anytime soon. But it buzzed as soon as I closed my eyes. There was an address. I didn't reply, I closed the phone and willed the flight to go fast.

When I landed there was another text waiting for me. It was a time and a geo location. I checked my watch. I had roughly thirty minutes to get to the location. Shit. There was no doubt in my mind I was going. I ran through the airport like a banshee on a mission, not sure what had gotten into me. The guy at the rental company probably stole my soul, but since it was on Eran's dime I didn't give fuck. A fiery death called for me as I weaved in and out of traffic trying to get to the spot. I didn't even know where I was going. There wasn't time to look it up.

With barely seconds to spare, I came to stop at a little place. It was a restaurant, but tiny. I double checked the location and it was correct. It was a little Indian place. I tried the door but it was locked. So I slipped my hands in my pockets. They were freezing. I hadn't remembered my gloves, and on a bike in this weather. My mother would have told me off. I spun around looking for a sign. Or even the telltale black SUV. There was nothing. The side street was deserted.

Xavier: I'm here.

A door opened behind me, and I turned to find Doug staring at me.

"He in there?"

Doug nodded. I stepped up to him and waited. He glared at me before stepping aside. It was dimly lit, candles flickering, not enough light to shine through the drapes. It truly looked closed. I moved further back into the place as Doug locked the door behind me.

Louis was sitting there in the back, in a booth, completely at ease. He held a glass of something and looked over as I approached.

"What is this?" I asked as I slipped into the other side of the booth.

"I thought we'd have dinner."

"Isn't this a bit of a risk?"

"Doug took care of it."

I knew what he must have meant. NDAs all around.

"Do this a lot do you?"

"This is a first, but my title has its uses." He set his drink down and leaned forward. "I hope you don't mind but I ordered while I waited. And my eyes are way larger than my stomach. Anne always makes fun of me."

I shrugged. I wasn't overly picky. I wasn't sure how this made me feel.

"Something to drink?" a waiter I hadn't noticed approach asked me.

I looked from him back to Louis. "What he's drinking."

"A gin and tonic." He half bowed to Louis and left.

"You know, I find it amusing half my country calls you Lewis."

"Damn Americans butcher everything."

"Louis." I said his name again, loving the way it sounded on my lips, like we Americans would say Louie. "It tastes sexual on the tongue. I rather like saying it whilst in bed."

I tried the name again, seeing how it tasted. "Louis."

"It sounds better on your lips with that damn accent."

I bought my fingers to my lip, and they found the scar there. They always found the scar. Rubbing my middle finger over it had become the worst nervous habit. As if subconsciously I wanted to draw more attention to the blight on my skin. I forced myself to stop, shoving my fingers into my hair instead.

He moved my hand, placing it on the table. "Don't hide your face."

"I wasn't."

He trailed his fingers over mine but pulled back his hand

when the waiter reappeared. He grabbed his drink and sipped as he sat back. The waiter kept his eyes downcast like he actually respected our privacy. I grabbed the gin and tonic and took a gulp.

"You don't have to stay."

"I'm a little surprised you don't have somewhere to be."

"We had downtime after traveling. But we're back to a full day tomorrow including dinner with the ambassador and visits to hospitals."

"I don't know how you do it."

"It's been this way as long as I could remember. My school photos were published in every magazine. I was at dinners with dignitaries as soon as I had table manners." He lifted one shoulder.

"Don't you hate it?"

"No." It was a simple answer.

"But there is no privacy."

"There is privacy in places. There isn't privacy in public, but I've adapted to it. For most, going out is a treat, my life is the opposite. I relish the time I get in private and those I get to spend it with."

"And what do you do when you stay in?"

"I read or play board games."

I laughed. "Board games, really?"

"Yes." There was a look in his eyes, like he was daring me to make fun of him.

"Like Risk, Monopoly, what?"

"I enjoy Risk, but it's not my favourite. There are some phenomenally made games. Like Forbidden Island, Pandemic, King of Tokyo…tons of them."

"I've never heard of any of those."

"They are quite popular."

"And who do you play these with?" I asked.

"My sister, family, friends." He lifted a shoulder, like it was nothing. But this wasn't something that could be read about him. It was something you'd have to have a conversation with him about, and I loved knowing little pieces of the real him. He told me more about his board games, which was hilariously adorable.

We were interrupted again by platters of food. There was curry and tandoori chicken, naan, tikka, and a lentil dish. He'd chosen well.

"I hope there is something to your taste."

"Plenty." I looked into his eyes and if he'd asked me to come home with him right then I would have. I was screwed.

What did a guy with tons of money and a title do for fun? Stay home.

"So you could go to any place in the world, have doors thrown open for you, go to the most exclusive places, and you prefer to stay in. Tell me why?" I knew I was pushing and prying but I selfishly wanted more.

He looked at me, really looked at me, pausing to finish chewing before he spoke. "No."

I was expecting more but he returned to eating and I was left wanting more. He was too good at that. "And why not?" I prompted.

He set down his fork and picked up his drink, slowly, alluringly slow, he brought it to his lips. "I don't like to explain it, and most people can't grasp it."

"Try me."

He crossed and uncrossed his ankle over his knee. "Being in public is work. I have to play a role and be this person I'm expected to be. It doesn't matter where I am. Even partying in Vegas I'd be this entity. More so because I have to hide what I am. So I'd rather spend the time I get to myself in."

My lips split into a smile against my will. I didn't want to enjoy his answer. "So the extroverted occupation is inhabited by an introvert."

"I guess you could look at it as such, or you could say I value my privacy."

"Well as a giant introvert who basically hates people or attention I feel you." I don't know why I said it. I hated talking about myself. I guess I felt comfortable with him, even though I didn't want to like him.

"But why?"

"Because people suck?"

"Your job is so public."

I pointed my fork at him. "Not as public as yours." I laughed. "Mine isn't public. Yes, I have to be outside and it's a drag, but I don't have to deal with people like you do. It's frankly as introverted as you can get and still be in public. I get to keep myself at a distance."

He looked like he was trying to hold back a laugh. "I guess it's a slight difference."

I flipped him off. "More than slight. I could never do what you do."

"I wasn't given a choice." Sorrow crept into his eyes. He masked it quickly and changed the subject which I wasn't going to press. "So when can I expect you to extract this pay back?"

"When I feel like it." I couldn't help but smirk. I rather liked having one over one him. "It's on my time."

He licked over his lips, and my eyes followed the path of his tongue. "If it's convenient and I can fit you into my schedule."

I sat forward placing my forearms on the table. "You made a deal. You owe me."

"I guess you'll have to give me some advance notice." He tossed his napkin on the table and sat back. "I'm a busy man."

Part of me knew it was an act, but too much of me wanted to demand repayment. "We have a deal, and I'll cash in on it when I see fit, and you'll make time for me."

"Demanding, aren't you?" There was a twinkle in his eyes.

"Don't push me or I'll do it tonight."

Doug came up alongside the table and tapped his watch.

"I should have time after my prior engagement." He slid out of the booth and stood.

"I'll be expecting a message when you finish up," I said, getting up myself.

Louis leaned in and whispered. "Remember how you asked me how I'd get you back into bed if I wanted you?

I nodded and swallowed hard.

"I'd do that." He pulled back as sly as a dog. He didn't wait for an answer either. He was gone like he'd never been there.

LOUIS

I felt pretty good about things. Much better than drunkenly texting him with no answer. I was getting to see him, and it was on my terms. It was dark. The dark that sets in in the winter and covers everything like a cold blanket. It wrapped up everything and clung to your bones. I had a large fire going in the hotel room, but it barely cut through the cold that clung to me after having spent the evening on an ice skating rink. He was going to show up. It would be any minute, and I hadn't been saying that since I arrived two hours ago.

I kicked my feet up and took another swallow of gin. Maybe cocky bastard hadn't been the way to go with Xavier. I could have misread the situation entirely, but I'd thought he'd enjoy the gesture. Maybe it was too desperate of a ploy.

Xavier: Send Doug.

Or maybe not.

I wanted to pace while Doug was fetching him. I wanted to get up, get him a drink, get naked, but I made myself sit there poised with my ankle over my knee and drink in hand, only lit by the fire in front of me. Minutes passed, each one feeling like an eternity, and I almost believed my watch stopped. At long last the lock clicked, and Xavier stepped into the light. He held a bag in one hand, and my heart picked up speed. An overnight bag perhaps, but as he stepped forward and set it on the table I saw it was a camera bag.

"Don't move," he said in a whisper.

"What are we doing?"

"I want these for me. I'll sign whatever you want so you know I'll keep them to myself, but I get a different you. One only I see, and I want it on film."

It was the most romantic thing someone had ever said to me.

"I want to be able to look at them and remember this. You."

"I want a copy."

"Sure." He brushed his fingers over the small of my back, sending a spark up my spine. "Now stand still."

I indulged him and stayed in place. He unzipped the bag and slid out his DSLR. He changed something and then held it up to his face and clicked the shutter. Taking a look at the screen, he moved ever so slightly to the left and held it to his face again.

"Look at the fire."

I did as I was told. He came close and moved my arm with the drink a fraction and placed my other arm over the back of the sofa.

Click. Click. Click.

He set the camera aside and took a seat on the edge of the

chair next to me.

"Done with my repayment so soon?"

There was a light in his eyes. "Not a chance." He looked me over, his eye stopping on the top two buttons of my shirt which remained undone. "But you'll want that photo. To release for something. You look too alluring and regal to not have it. It was more for you than for me."

I was shocked. "Let me see."

He picked up the camera again and leaned closer to me to show me the screen. I looked like something out of a novel. Mysterious and alluring. I liked it. And I didn't like many photos of myself.

"You're quite talented."

He sat back, keeping the camera in his lap. "How much liberty are you giving me?"

I mirrored him and looked him over, taking my time with my answer. "Why are you asking?"

Lust crossed through his gaze. "Take off the shirt."

I obliged him, slowly working my fingers down the buttons. I slid it off and set it aside. He looked me over, hungry. My cock stirred at the look. I'd never felt so desired by another person. He slid forward on the seat and brought the camera back to his face. I stayed as I was until he told me to move.

"Sit on the edge of the table," he said breathless.

I was glad this was getting to him as much as it was me. It was entirely foreign to give someone such a thing over me. To allow someone to take these photos. It was daring and exhilarating. I'd have to be careful or I'd get addicted to the acting out like some bored teenager.

I sat on the edge of the table closest to the fire, and he moved back to take a few shots. I looked up when he hadn't said anything in a few moments to find him just watching me. The fire illuminated his scar, and I wanted to kiss the length of it, from his brow to his lips. I licked my lip and my chest rose as I inhaled fully, trying to calm myself. He snapped another photo.

"What do you see?" I asked, unable to stand wondering a moment longer. I wanted to know how he saw me.

"I see hunger," he said as he came closer. "The way you look at me." The camera hung at his side as he stalked closer.

I wanted to reach out for him. To shove him into the chair he'd occupied and climb on top of him, but I refrained because more than wanting him, I wanted to see what he did.

"Take your pants off."

I raised a brow but didn't say more.

"You told me I could get what I wanted," he said, not allowing me to question his tone.

So I did what he asked. I stripped off my slacks and tossed them to where my shirt lay. He took another photo before I could sit.

"No, stay there."

So I did. His fingers brushed over my shoulder, in the lightest touches urging me to move this way and that, leaving a trail of heat each place he touched. All the while the camera was in his hand and he was working the shutter. I watched him, lust pouring out of me. I expected it to be fully visible in each and every photo. If these photos were ever released...I couldn't imagine. Sure they were still tame. I was standing in my boxers, and other royals had done much worse, but there was more there. He was there. Not visible in the photos, but I would always know when I looked at them.

He dropped to his knees in front of me, looking up at me through his dark lashes, and I couldn't stop the groan that slipped from my lips. My cock had gone from half hard to fully tenting my boxer briefs in that instant, and there would be no mistaking it in any photos taken from here forward.

He watched me as he slipped a single finger into the waistband of my undergarments. He paused, waiting for me to say no. No words came. Even if I'd wanted to speak, my mouth was too dry. My tongue was stuck where it was.

He tugged them lower on the v of my hips, exposing the close cut hair there. And the camera I'd almost forgotten was back in place in front of his face. He pulled until the base of my cock was exposed, and then took a picture. I was trying to summon some type of sentence, anything at all. I didn't want him to stop, but I should tell him to.

He moved the camera and pressed his lips near his finger and kissed. Gooseflesh raised where I felt him. Hot and wet. He trailed his lips towards my dick. Nothing in the world felt so good. He moved my shorts even lower, exposing the rest of me. And the camera was back, but instead of pressing it to his face he held it up for me to take as he gripped my base with his free hand. He moved his mouth to my tip and looked up at me waiting.

I took the camera from him and he smiled. "Now take the pictures you want to keep," he said before taking me into his mouth.

I forgot about what was in my hand for a long moment as I watched his lips take me in. My breath hitched, and I memorised every line in his face and then realised I didn't have to. I lifted the camera and he grinned around me. I nearly died right there.

The need in his eyes, and the way he looked in the firelight. I took more than one picture as he continued, and it seemed to egg him on. He squeezed my base and took more of me into his mouth and throat.

Bloody hell, I wished he was naked. I wanted more pictures. I wanted to take them and then I wanted to look at them again before we fucked.

His tongue stroked the underside of my cock and my head fell back.

"Take your clothes off," I demanded.

He looked up at me, his dark eyes glinting in the fire light. "Look at you ordering me around." But he backed off my cock and climbed to his feet and pushed his jeans and boxers off in one motion. He stood there as if waiting, and I remembered the camera. A smile licked at my lips as I took a few shots of him, and then he was on me. He raked his nails over my back as our bodies met. I grabbed his ass and found his mouth. I could taste my precum on his lips, and I wanted him back there.

"Your shirt?" I fingered the material.

"It isn't pretty." He looked down, embarrassed. "I don't want to ruin this." When he looked back to gage my reaction I caught his lips in a kiss.

"Please."

He nodded and grabbed the back of his shirt and pulled it off. The scar on his face extended down from his shoulder to the middle of his abs. The skin hadn't been placed back together well, or it had become infected. It was wilted and probably restitched, leaving the area marred.

His chest rose and fell as he breathed, stretching and pulling the scar.

"You're even more beautiful than I imagined." It was the truth. I placed my lips to the beginning of the scar on his collarbone. "Will you tell me how it happened?"

"Maybe." He pressed his body to mine, and his fingers caressed my obliques.

I wasn't going to push it and ruin the moment. I wanted this moment, so I switched gears, thankful he'd given me what he had.

"Suck my cock."

"I like the filthy mouthed prince," he said, shoving me into a seat on the sofa.

I spread my knees and waited for him. He eagerly took me back in his mouth, and I relaxed back to enjoy it.

"Don't you dare come," he warned as he gripped my balls.

I moaned my answer, not sure I was quite coherent and not caring. But he was too good at this, and my gut turned as I fought back my release.

"X…" I moaned.

He slowed and looked up. "You're too easy." He licked his lips as he stood. "I want your ass, and I want pictures of me inside you.

The well-trained part of me screamed no, but I silenced it and nodded. "What are you waiting for?"

He dug in a side pocket of his bag and pulled out a condom and lube.

I was impressed. "You came prepared."

"I came here with bad intentions."

It had worked. This was what I'd wanted when I'd invited him to dinner. Lust raged through my blood. I loved that I could do this to him.

"By design." I watched as he rolled the latex over himself.

"Planned all this, did you?" He stroked over himself and my mouth watered. I suddenly regretted not having had a turn with him in my mouth before I'd let him put a condom on.

"I wanted you again." It was simple and the truth.

"You must be easy to impress." He looked me over, like he could devour me with his eyes. "Turn around."

I did as he asked, kneeling on the sofa. His fingers trailed down the split of my arse. "Now this is lovely."

I knew he was mocking me, but I rather enjoyed it. His slick fingers found my opening. He wasn't gentle, and I didn't want him to be. I wanted him just to take me already. I pushed back on to his fingers and moaned. "Fuck me."

I heard the click of his shutter as his head pressed into me. I closed my eyes as everything in me screamed not to let him do this, while my dick with a mind of its own, begged for more. I wanted to see how he looked stretching me and taking me. He slid forward, and I risked a glance, watching as he leaned back to get the best angle of himself. There was pleasure written in his looks. I wanted him to look at me like that forever.

"Don't worry. There are none of your face." He tossed the camera to the sofa beside me and hooked his fingers around my hips. "That way you have deniability."

I turned away from him and smiled to myself. I didn't get to enjoy the sentiment long because he slammed into me, and

I had to stroke myself or my dick was going to fall off.

"I want to feel you come while I'm inside you."

"Keep talking." I didn't know where this was coming from. I usually topped, and I rarely let anyone order me around, but the way he did it. I moaned. I couldn't get enough.

He smacked my ass. "Like that do you?"

"Yes." I met his thrusts, stroking myself in rhythm.

"I'm going to own you all night long, so when you're sitting on your pompous ass tomorrow you're going to think of me."

"You want me to be thinking about you in my arse."

I knew I got to him by the sounds he made. His dick twitched in my arse, and I looked at him over my shoulder.

"Harder."

He smacked my arse again, and I hoped there would be a mark where his handprint burned into my muscle.

"More." I was going to egg him on until he gave me what I wanted.

He pressed forward filling me with every inch of himself so he was pressed into my back, and his lips found my neck.

He whispered, "You want marks, don't you?"

I panted out a yes, wrapping an arm around his back to keep him there.

We writhed together, and his mouth moved along the curve of my neck where it met my shoulder. He wasn't gentle though. He bit down, and it pushed me over the edge.

We fucked off and on like teenagers, the unspoken need to get it out of our system because we both knew this couldn't continue. And maybe, just maybe if we exhausted ourselves of each other we'd wake up not wanting it tomorrow. It was a lie, but a lie we needed to convince ourselves of.

I laid there watching him come down within arm's reach of me. We were both still panting. I'd lost count of how many times we'd fucked. Maybe it would be enough for the spank bank during the long dry years.

I had a duty.

I had a duty.

Maybe if I kept repeating it to myself it would wash away everything else. Or maybe I'd keep picking up my phone to text Xavier when I knew I shouldn't be. We could be friends, right? I could behave myself.

"Sorry, I've been wanting to do that since dinner, and I couldn't stop myself." He pushed a hand into his hair. "It won't happen again."

I turned to look into his eyes. We'd made it to the bed at some point, and he was sprawled out there, and I had to stop myself from touching him again. My cock needed a few minutes to recover.

"What if I wanted it to happen again?" The words were out of my mouth before I could swallow them.

"We both know—"

I cut him off with my fingers on his lips. "I'm here a few more weeks. What if we play until I go home? We clearly work well together." I had something here. Who were we hurting? He bit my finger, and I groaned. "Don't start, hear me out."

"Maybe I'm trying to shut you up." He flicked his tongue over my fingers, and my cock started to get hard again.

"You have quite the stamina."

"I could say the same to you." When I tried to pull back my hand he caught it with his.

"It's been building for some time," I admitted. "We aren't hurting anyone."

"And what do you propose? I sneak up here every night and we fuck?"

"And more. I like your mind as well. You know, to entertain me between rounds."

He laughed. "Right, because you could have anyone you wanted up here to fuck."

"I could, but I want you."

"Why me? Why not Drake?"

I slid a hand around to the small of his back. "You're the most beautiful man I've ever laid eyes on."

He laughed.

"I'm not joking."

He rolled his eyes and shook his head, but I went on.

"And I trust you, which I've never found in someone I was sleeping with."

His brow creased in the centre, and he tensed under me.

"Don't overthink it, but it's true."

He grabbed hold of my arse. "It's sad. I'm not overthinking it. You deserve to be happy and not worry."

"Easier said than done."

"So what are we going to do between romps? Are you going to teach me your board games?" He rolled on top of me, and I opened my thighs for him.

"But of course. I'm going to school your arse in them."

He dipped his head, tasting my throat. "How does this work then?"

"Well I was hoping you'd stay the night."

"I think that can be arranged, and then what?" he asked.

"Then we go back to what we've been doing."

"Except you come up here at night."

I could see him thinking it over, and I wasn't sure he would go for it. I mean, what did I have to offer? Lots of secret sex? Him getting to feel like I was hiding him? Even if he understood the reasons, it wasn't an easy thing to expect of someone, and I would fully understand when he said no.

"At least stay tonight, even if you have to be gone tomorrow."

XAVIER

I didn't answer. I kissed him and kissed him and kissed him again. I knew what he was asking me to do. Be his forever secret. Share these few weeks, and then go back to what? Texting? Nothing? Pretending we were strangers. Even if we could see each other again, once he left here we could never be this again. He couldn't afford to. Once he returned, he was going to have to get serious about a wife and an heir, and I wasn't going to want to watch.

The thought of being there for him and encouraging him to be with someone else made my insides turn. I'd fully admit there were stronger people than I to be able to pine and not have. So I'd do this, but I was going to tell him we had to cut off all contact after he left. I'd change my number and vanish from his life. It was the only way I could do it.

So I didn't answer. I kissed him and fucked him, and then held him while he slept, coming to terms with the gravity of what I was going to do. Because I rarely liked anyone. I was really damn good at my introverting and keeping people at a distance, but once I let someone in, they were in. They got a piece of my cold dead heart. So I'd give him that piece and then I'd cut it out of my chest when he left. Easy right?

No, because the reality of it was I was someone to warm his bed, but to me it was so much more.

I woke to an empty bed. I rolled to my side and looked at the clock. It was three-thirty in the morning. There was no way he was getting up for his day yet, so where had he gone? I closed my eyes, willing myself to go back to sleep, but my brain was slipping into overdrive. If I wasn't going to go back to sleep I wasn't going to lay there and think.

I made myself roll out of bed and go in search of him. The room was black, and I was going to run into something. I needed to find my phone. I thought I'd left it on the table, but who really knew at this point. I started to walk in the general direction, going slow so I didn't end up with bruised shins. But something outside caught my attention, and there he was, standing there in just boxer briefs looking out over the city.

I watched him for a few minutes before I crossed the room and slid open the door. I was hit with a cool blast of wind and didn't know how Louis was standing it in so few clothes. I stepped outside and closed the door behind me, wrapping my arms around my middle to attempt to stay warm. Noticing my posture, Louis turned and flipped on a heater he was standing next to. I stepped under the rays making the weather tolerable.

"What are you doing out here?"

"Thinking," was the only thing he said and went back to peering over the side.

"About?" I asked.

"Life, the universe, and everything."

I laughed. "Adams. Funny. The answer is forty-two."

"But what does that mean?"

"I guess we'll never know as the Earth gets destroyed before the program finishes."

"And isn't that a metaphor for our lives?"

"We die before we figure out our purpose?" I asked.

He smiled and then went back to gazing over the edge. I didn't expect him to say anything else but he did. "You're going to be gone in the morning, aren't you?"

"Do you really think this is a good idea?" I asked. Because I didn't.

"No, but I don't want to stop. I've never been allowed to be selfish, and it feels like this is my one opportunity to make myself happy."

"Even if there is an end date?" He was breaking my cold dead heart a little.

He looked over at me. "It's better to have loved and lost than to have never loved at all." There was a lingering smirk to his lips as he continued the quotes.

"I need some cynical bastard quote about the pain never being worth it. I'm not good at this." I scrunched up my forehead, trying to think.

"You're not really as cynical as you claim to be."

I scoffed and challenged him, "How do you know?"

"I can see through it. It's an act you use so you aren't rejected."

I didn't want him to be right. I wanted to be a child and retort a whatever. "It's easier than putting myself out there. I don't disappoint myself."

"Don't you want more?" he asked me.

"Do you want to live vicariously through me or something?"

"I don't get more." He sighed and turned towards me. "I get to be this womanizing bastard to keep my image intact, and then I get to propose to some woman I'll probably have my sister choose to get it to look like a fairytale because it's good for the country's morale."

"Maybe you should come out."

"It would never be allowed."

I was sad for him. "Renounce your claim or whatever you would have to do. You can't live with a woman. It's not fair to her, and it's not fair to you."

"I'll have to tell her. I'm sure even if I was honest with them I'd still have a line of people willing to do it." He was probably right. But it didn't make it okay. "It would disqualify me from secession if I came out as gay, probably. It's up to Parliament."

"Why won't you disqualify yourself then?"

He looked at me and looked away again. Like he couldn't look me in the eyes as he poured out his pain. "Because I couldn't do that to Anne. She doesn't want it, never has, and if she had to, the stress alone would probably make her relapse."

"Rock and a hard place."

He nodded and didn't say more. But it wasn't okay. He shouldn't have to miss out on love and more because he was protecting his sister. I wanted to say so, but I doubted he'd listen to it coming from me. So I stayed quiet. But maybe I shouldn't. Maybe I should press it. I didn't know him well, but with as shitty as gays were treated, maybe a gay prince would do a load of good. I was torn.

He trailed his fingers up my arm, pulling my attention to him. "I have to be up early. Come back to bed."

"As a guy you're just fucking it's probably not my place to say this, but you should come out eventually. It would do the world of good for our rights and kids. You could show a lot of kids it's okay to be who you are."

He looked at me long and hard, and frankly I was expecting him to kick me out or something by the expression he wore. "Why do I have to carry that burden? And then what if I do it and they disqualify me? I gave to protect Anne. I swore I would when my parents died. Her life has already been too hard."

He was right. Why should that fall to him, and it was noble what he was doing for his sister, but it was still shit. He slid his fingers into mine and tugged me towards the door. I followed willingly.

XAVIER

Just like that we fell into a sort of rhythm. I'd wake up as he was getting ready for his day and lay in bed watching him. Then I'd meander around making extra money by taking photos around the studios.

"You are entirely lazy," Louis said one morning after about a week of our new routine. He was tying his tie in the mirror and looking at me through it.

"You wish you could be this lazy." I rubbed my hands over the sheets and then flipped over, putting my ass in the air for his viewing pleasure.

"Cruel, so cruel."

"Leering isn't very princely," I said with a yawn.

"Says who?"

I looked over my shoulder at him, his eyes still on my ass. "Tis a shame you don't have more time."

"I'll have my way with your arse tonight."

"If I'm here." I laid my head on the pillow, waiting for his reaction.

"What else would you have going on?" he said through gritted teeth.

I shrugged and stretched out further. "I could catch a show, get called in to work, or perhaps go out."

"You hate people." He sounded offended, and I rather loved it.

"What's your point?"

"You would rather go out than come here?"

I yawned and glanced back again. "Was I invited? I don't know your schedule."

"I've made sure to be here."

I didn't know where this was coming from. Maybe I was expecting him to get bored. "I know."

He came over and sat on the edge of the bed. "Is this wearing on you?" He trailed his fingers down my spine.

I rolled over, capturing his hand with mine and bringing it to my lips. "No, I'm all good, Louis."

He replaced his hands with his lips. "Have I told you how much I enjoy it when you say my name?"

"Is that so, Louis?"

"Mmmhmm," he moaned. "It's exquisite on your lips."

"Be late," I urged, knowing it was impossible. Not only would it be incredibly rude to whatever charity or state event he was going to, but people would start asking questions.

"I can't."

"What, will Doug drag you out by the balls?"

"I wouldn't put it past him. He's ruthless with my schedule."

"Now I want to keep you here just to see it." I looped my

fingers under his belt and dragged him into bed.

"Are you trying to make me look like I've just had a romp in the back of my car?"

"Mmmm. I would enjoy the questions that raised." I sucked his lower lip into my mouth.

"I'm sure you would, evil bastard."

I started to pull his shirt out of the back of his pants grinning up at him. "Just suck my dick before you go."

"And get cum on my tie?"

I licked over my lips. "Why does everything sound so much better and filthier coming from your mouth?"

"Because our accent is far superior."

I slipped my hand into the back of his bespoke slacks and dug my nails into his ass. "Proper filthy eh?" I said in a mock accent.

"We don't say eh."

"It fit."

"I am not Canadian."

"Close enough."

"Americans." He took a kiss, and I completely forgot everything we'd been talking about as his tongue caressed over mine.

"You even taste British," I said as he pulled back.

He was up and fixing himself. I sighed and tucked my hands under my head.

"Tonight then?" Louis asked.

"Am I going get you in the daylight at some point?"

Doug stepped into the room just then. I grabbed the sheet to pull over my dick and put my arm over my face. I was glad at that moment there was an expiration date. I couldn't imagine feeling like we were always being watched by someone. I valued my privacy too much, but then when I thought of not coming back tonight I couldn't bring myself to do it.

The prince looked up from slipping on his jacket and looked from me to Doug.

Doug balked and gestured with his hands. "We'll have to look at the schedule. Maybe your sister could cover something."

He walked back over to me purposefully and leant down to brush his lips over mine. "I'll make it happen."

I closed my eyes, melting into his kiss. It wasn't going to happen, but the sentiment was nice. When he pulled back, I slipped my fingers into his hair and took more.

Doug cleared his throat, but Louis ignored him, which made me smile. By the time we were done he had to fix his clothes again. Another thing that made me smile.

Doug nodded as he walked out behind the prince. I was alone in the room with one of the other body men who would stay until I left. It made me wonder if we prolonged this how many empty promises there would be. I could imagine a lifetime of empty promises as I lived in a flat close to the palace. Part of me hungered for it, even if it was scarce nights until he got bored of me.

I couldn't show him the weakness in my resolve or he'd capitalize on it. Who would blame him? I didn't want to be Drake. I didn't want to be a mistress.

I had to get out of this room before it made me crazy. With his damn smell lingering everywhere I was going insane. I hadn't talked to Eran yet, but I was sure whatever he had for me was of low importance, or trash. Neither would net me a ton of cash, and it was just to fill my time.

So I'd drink coffee and read emails, naked, in the luxury suite because it was probably the only time in my life I was going to get to put my balls on expensive furniture.

I got out my laptop and decided to look at the photos I'd taken of the prince. I'd just kicked my feet up on the table, about to shove a muffin in my face when my cell started to ring. So much for enjoying those pictures again. I'd been enjoying them a lot while he did his duty.

"Hollo?" I mumbled chewing my muffin.

"Ignore the email I sent," Eran said.

"Okay…"

"You haven't looked at it yet?"

"Nope." He knew I wasn't an early riser.

"Anyway, it's fine. I have something big for you."

Now I was interested. "Give it to me."

"I have a lead on a room that looks into the Prince's suite, and I've been told there has been someone in there with him."

I whipped around looking for open curtains as I sat here with my balls out. "What?" I had a big issue not sputtering. If we'd been on FaceTime the gig would be up. I was sure guilty was written all over me.

"Are you that surprised? Don't all the royals sleep around?" Eran laughed, but it was an awkward laugh like he was trying to make me more at ease because he sensed there was something off.

"Yes and no. You'd think someone in his position would be more careful." I tried to sound like I was shrugging it off. What the hell had we done at the windows? I couldn't even think. I should know to be careful, and I hadn't been.

"You know as well as I do we get our best shots when people get too comfortable."

His words struck a cord with me. They made me feel wrong. I wanted to puke, and my chest constricted.

"The room is already paid for, we can't be behind on this."

I wanted to say I'd rather not, but then how would I look? I also couldn't say there was no way you'd catch the guy…or girl, but again he'd want to know how I knew such things. But it was going to be a big waste of time for everyone involved. He was paying for me to be here. I couldn't say no.

"I'm on it." It was time to talk to Louis, and I knew that conversation wouldn't go well.

LOUIS

"What's next?" It had been a particularly early morning after a late night, and I wanted to drown myself in coffee until I had to put my princely face back on and venture back out into public. So I was hoping for a meal off, but I'd been too brain-dead this morning when Grace had shoved the schedule under my nose.

"You have a lunch."

I groaned. "Please tell me it's not something I have to be intellectual at?"

She wrinkled her nose and pushed her glasses up. She reminded me of my primary school librarian who would shhh me and give me a death stare any time I opened my mouth during silent reading. So when Grace spoke, I shut up.

"I'm not sure who put this here. Hmmmm." She looked at it again. "Where's Anne? It's something with Anne, but I don't remember putting anything here."

"Anne had me put it on the Prince's schedule." Doug

walked up to the car we stood outside. "He had the lunch free, and she wanted the time since they've barely crossed paths in the last week."

Grace looked over the rim of her glasses at Doug. A silent scold.

Doug appeared to not notice. "We'll meet you at the next event."

She cocked her head. "Well."

It was pretty clear she was offended as she was used to being my shadow.

"Don't worry about it, Grace. She probably just wants some privacy."

"You know I can't handle things unless I know what's going on." She hedged, like Doug would give something away.

I chuckled turning up the charm. "It's lunch with my sister."

She walked off in a huff, and Doug got in the driver's seat and I got in the back.

"Why is she in a tiff over lunch with Anne?" I asked.

Doug lifted one shoulder but looked like there was more he wasn't saying.

"Come on."

"Anne made her and a lot of the staff's lives difficult. She will never complain, but she doesn't want you to get wrapped up in anything Anne. When she found out you two snuck off to the club she was livid. Fretting for days over if it would come out. She was protective over your parents too, and she wants the best for you."

And suddenly I felt bad for what I was doing, because if it

ever did come out I would be just another stain on the Gotha name. I had to push it out of my head. I couldn't think about it and keep doing what I was, and I was going to keep doing it.

"I can't just stop seeing my sister."

"We know. Doesn't mean there aren't feelings, but it's not lunch with Anne you're going to anyway. She took the rest of the day off."

I was sure the confusion was showing on my face.

"He told me not ta tell ya, but I will."

"What did he do?" I asked, unable to hide the smile that came to my lips.

"He asked me if you had time today, and well you had lunch so I had Anne put herself on your schedule."

"Where are we going?" My dick was already half hard in anticipation. I prayed it was to the hotel for a quickie.

"He planned lunch for you two. Romantic," he said the last in a mocking tone.

"Please, if you could get a girlfriend you'd kill for the romance."

"I'd be the romance." He looked back at me in the review mirror.

I rolled my eyes. "If you're so romantic, why are you single?"

He gave me a flat look. "Because I'm always working for this prick."

I gave him a finger, glad the windows were tinted. Grace would have a cow if a picture of me using such a gesture got out. When we pulled up at the hotel, I looked at Doug, confused.

"It's up there."

It would have been nice to go out, but I figured it was probably better to eat take away in the room. And it warmed my heart that he understood these things. And I liked being alone with him. As much as I would have liked to show him off in public, which would never happen, my life was public, so having something that was just mine made me happy.

When I opened the door to my suite, he was laying on his side on a blanket. The take away all set up like a picnic on the floor.

"I thought about being naked when you walked in, but since Doug did me a solid bringing you back here, I thought I'd be nice and not make him look at my dick."

Doug looked at the ceiling and muttered something incoherent before walking out of the room.

"I'm sure that was a thanks," I lied, as I crossed the room and took a seat on the edge of the blanket.

"Hey," he said. He started to open the take away, and it put tiny cracks in my heart.

The worst part about meeting the perfect person was knowing it and knowing I couldn't keep him. I could see him in the palace with me. I could see him playing board games with Anne and I, and I could see fucking him senseless every time we were alone. I'd have to live the rest of my life knowing he existed and I couldn't have him.

"Is this okay?"

"It's wonderful," I said taking the plate he offered.

"Then why do you look like someone just kicked your puppy?"

I schooled my face and shook my head. "It's just nice. I don't think you understand. Anyone else would have wanted to take me out and be seen with me, and here I ask you to be my secret fuck buddy, and you're so much more. You're a friend and you surprise me with take away."

"My intentions were entirely selfish. You're giving me too much credit." He looked down at the food avoiding my eyes, and I knew he was lying.

"I don't believe you for a minute."

"I wanted to fuck the princeling. How is that not selfish?"

"Because you get me off just as good as you take." I let him have his denial. It was better for both of us.

XAVIER

Laying in bed in the bliss of sex, I still had Eran's call weighing on me. Louis rolled to his side still breathing hard. We had been quite acrobatic in the short time we'd had. I looked over at him as his fingers stroked up my arm.

The way he looked at me was going to put me in an early grave. I'd never felt so much from just one look. And I had to crush him.

"I'll be done around nine tonight, but I was thinking, I know my schedule is tightly packed, but maybe I could feign sick and work a day in so we can stay in bed." He was entirely too cute when he was rambling, and I didn't want to send him crashing, but I didn't know how to break it to him.

"Do you think you'd actually be able to pull off a whole day?" Maybe he wouldn't notice I was avoiding.

"I'm going to see what we can cancel. The Queen did promise me some downtime while we were here, and since we went to Chicago there hasn't been anything."

"You got duped."

"More like they didn't realize how packed we'd be."

"Too true."

"Grace doesn't like to say no to anyone either."

"Grace?" I asked.

"She's my social secretary. She's always on a mission to get me as much good press as possible. I think after all the Anne stuff she's high-strung."

"She worried you'll come out as gay or something?" I said trying not to laugh.

"She's got no idea, but I'm sure she thinks I'll end up naked in Vegas and all over the papers."

"It's already happened, how bad could it be?" I felt guilty not telling him after the turn the conversation took.

"I'm sure she has some worse scenario stuck in her head."

"Like us being seen on your balcony?" I asked and regretted the words as soon as they came out.

"Well if she knew about us I'm sure... wait."

"Yeah, I got a call from Eran this morning. There are grainy photos someone is claiming is us. Since it's your floor and your hotel, which clearly is verifiable, it's pretty good odds it's us, unless you've been sneaking someone else up here while I'm sleeping."

He laughed without humor. "You can't be serious."

"It's my job, and I'm here telling you about it."

"How many times have we been on the balcony?" He was rubbing a hand over his face and clearly worried.

"I doubt there are any clear pictures or they'd be running them, not putting me on it."

"But someone saw us, and there will be rumors."

I nodded. "Yeah, and I'm going to have to sit there all night."

Anger flashed over his face, but in an instant it was good. He was too good at schooling his emotions. "So when do I get you?"

"Are you mad there are rumors, or that we won't get any time?" I couldn't help but smile a little as I asked.

"Both. I've grown quite accustomed to getting my time." He pulled me closer and grabbed a hold of my ass.

I pressed into him. "I guess we'll have to figure out some alternatives in your schedule. I'm here aren't I?"

"Let me talk to Doug."

"Okay." I brushed my lips over his.

"What did your boss say about the rumors?"

"Nothing about it being a man, if you're worried about that. But of course they'd want pictures either way. If you're dating someone, it's news."

"But of course."

"Maybe you should get someone in here to fake date. Is that a thing you do?"

"Never. I always let the papers assume by the way I acted out." He sucked on my lower lip.

"Well maybe you should consider it to put this to bed."

He pulled back and studied my face. "No, we'll avoid the balcony and leave it at rumors. I'm not willing to do that to…" He didn't finish his sentence, leaving me wondering who he couldn't do that to?

Probably whatever girl who would take the fall and be relentlessly stalked by the press. He was a good guy at heart, which made it harder when I had to leave that morning, knowing I wouldn't be back for days at best.

LOUIS

"It's been three days. How much longer do you think he's going to keep you on this?" I'd broken down and called Xavier between events.

"Where are you?" he asked, ignoring my question.

I looked at Doug. "Where are we going?"

"To some cultural performance put on by children." He shrugged. "Grace has the schedule in the other car. I don't right remember."

"Oh, it's at the heritage museum."

Xavier laughed. "And then?"

I put my hand over my eyes and rubbed my temples. "Then it's a meeting at the council for indigenous relations. All great stuff."

"But it's going to be a long day?"

"Yes, quite long. I have this thing about kids performing."

"Kids performing? Like it creeps you out?" There was amusement in his tone.

"No, like I, well…I don't enjoy it."

"It's like nails on a chalkboard, isn't it?"

I sighed. "Yes, it's something I could imagine their parents love, but why do they make the rest of us listen?"

Xavier burst out laughing. "Parents are blind to those things. They think their kid is the greatest gift to the earth and everyone should see it."

"Exactly, but just wait, I'm sure I'll be the same."

Xavier got quiet, and I wondered if talking about what my life was going to be like in the future got to him. It got to me enough where I didn't think about it bothering him. It was just this eventuality I was going to have to deal with, and I was just going to have to treat it like any other aspect of the job.

"Back to the topic at hand, when am I going to get to see you?" I thought it best if I changed directions.

"Well since I'm stuck here all night, and you have packed days, I'm not sure."

I groaned to myself. "My dick is going to fall off."

"Can you say dick out loud?"

"It's just my body men in the car. I'm not worried about them." And I wasn't. Doug had known my preferences for some time.

"Well unless we can have a quickie between your schedule, we're going to have to wait Eran out."

I looked at Doug. "Any time today?"

"You barely have time to breathe, your highness."

"I heard him." There was as much defeat in his voice as I felt.

I love my country, I closed my eyes and started to say it on repeat.

"So then, when you're off. Hopefully he won't want to keep footing the bill if it leads to nothing."

"Hopefully." He sounded dejected, and it broke a part of me I didn't know existed.

This was even more evidence why love wasn't in the cards for me. Better to find someone for the job, as that's what being married to me would be. And I had to make sure they understood what it would be.

We hung up, and I wondered if I'd see him again. It would be smart for him to run far and fast. I was nothing but work, and there was no way the quality of the fuck made up for it. We parked, and I took a moment to compose myself.

As soon as I was in the venue I remembered why I loved my job and title. The children were so excited and pleased to see me. It was a wonder they knew who I was at all, and most of them were articulate and well educated. Part of my mind remained on Xavier, and I blamed my lack of hook ups for it because I didn't want to admit that I missed his company as well.

The children were pretty good, much to my surprise, and adorable. They were excited to put on a show they'd been practicing for months, and I didn't have a hard time staying focused, even as my mind tried to wander. Then as I was walking down the hall towards the reception I caught a glimpse of someone. Xavier? His name was on my lips, but I bit it back. It couldn't be.

Only event photographers and the ones on my staff were here. My brain must have been playing tricks on me. I was led around the corner towards the reception room, and there he was in the hall.

I blanched. How should I act? I looked around for witnesses, and only Doug was there, grinning like the bastard he was.

"You?" I asked him.

He lifted a shoulder. "He was already in here. I just helped with the bare hallway."

"How long do we have?" I asked as I bolted as nonchalantly as I could towards Xavier.

He checked his watch. "Maybe fifteen minutes before they'll start wondering where you are. Everyone poops."

"Great, that's what I want on the front of the papers. Prince gets the shits during heritage event."

Doug grinned. "Wouldn't be the first time a royal has been held up in the bathroom after lunch in a foreign country."

I slipped my hand around Xavier's hip as I stepped into him. "Thank you, Doug."

"Please don't make me watch," he said, deadpan.

"Now I feel a little bad about teasing him." Xavier gave him a grin.

He wrapped one of his large hands around the back of my neck and brought me in for a kiss. My lips met his, but I was sure he could tell how tentative I was. His taste lured me in, and for a few fleeting moments I forgot who I was. I pressed my body into his, pinning him to the wall as we kissed.

"You act like it's been more than two days," he said between kisses.

"It feels like it's been an eternity."

He nodded, rubbing his nose over mine. It was like a switch had been flipped. It was intense as ever, but slower, more passionate.

"I really don't want to have to stand here," Doug said, reminding us he was there. "And it's probably not safe."

He was right, but I couldn't stop touching him. His dick was so hard against mine. I was dying to be able to feel it. Him.

"Let's find someplace to be alone," Xavier said as he grabbed my arse.

"Way to make it impossible for me to think," I groaned into his lips.

He used the hand to leverage more friction as he ground into me. "Having a hard time focusing, Princeling?"

My eyes snapped open. "This princeling thing needs to go. Where did it even come from?"

"I feel like it's a mixture between duckling and prince. It's fitting, isn't it?"

"No." I shoved him back into the wall. "Why am I a duckling?"

He rebounded with a grunt but kept touching me, and we were back to kissing. "So worldly but so innocent. Look at you all nervous about making out in a hall. Something children do."

"Royals don't do PDA."

"Oh? Is that so? You seem to be doing just fine." He flipped us, slamming me into the wall.

My body responded to his roughness. "Where can we go?" I looked between the two of them.

"There is a loo over there." Doug pointed, and before I could respond, Xavier was pulling me towards it.

"The loo, really?" I said breathless. "If there are any papers with this…"

"Beggars can't be choosers," Xavier said as he pushed me

back towards the lavatories. "And you're going to have to be quiet."

"Is there a lock on the door?" I asked as he shoved me inside.

"Yes, you're lucky they have the single occupant washrooms in this building."

"You've no idea. I think I'd risk a broom cupboard at this point."

He was undressing me before the door was even fully closed behind us. He kicked it the rest of the way and took one hand off me to get the lock before renewing his vigour to get me out of my slacks.

"How can we possibly fuck in here?" I looked around for any possible surface.

"I don't have to fuck you." His eyes were alight with lust, and I could have come right there.

"Then what?"

He dropped to his knees, slipping a hand into my briefs as he did. "Don't worry. I think you'll be able to come."

And his mouth was almost better than sex. He pushed my head past his pale pink lips, and the visual alone. I groaned, and he looked up at me with a wry smile.

"I know," I whispered, but how could I stay silent with Xavier on his knees.

He moaned around my dick, and I needed to brace myself against something. I grabbed him by the hair and turned us around so I could lean back against the door. My knees were weak as pleasure washed over me.

He seemed to like my hands in his hair, so I tightened my grip, earning another moan.

My head dropped back against the door with a bang, and his eyes flashed up to meet mine. "Your highness needs to learn to be quiet."

I nodded, not sure I could make sense with words as he took me back into his mouth. There were voices outside, but they didn't stop Xavier. He kept going. The voices were getting closer, like a group had decided this out of the way hall was perfect to venture down right at this moment. I pulled at his head, but he wouldn't let up. I bit down on my lip, mostly stifling my moans.

"You're going to kill me," I hissed.

This seemed to delight him. He brought his free hand up and squeezed my balls. I whimpered, my knees starting to give. The chatter was passing us, and fear as well as excitement pumped through my veins. They couldn't get in here, fine, but we were going to have to leave at some point. What if we were heard and they waited around to see who'd been shagging in the bathroom?

And something clicked inside me. It was like I couldn't get enough of it. The fear made the pleasure so much more intense. I almost lost it down Xavier's throat right there. I wanted more and more.

Someone tried the handle and I gasped. They had to have heard me. My toes curled, and I didn't want it to stop. Xavier twisted his mouth and his hand in the opposite direction while swirling his tongue around the underside of my cock, and I lost it.

Ecstasy washed over me, and I bit down on my knuckle trying to fight back the sounds escaping my throat. I came and came and came. Never before in my life had something been this intense. This long, this powerful.

I was staggering when Xavier pulled off. He wore a huge shit eating grin and must have known what he did to me.

"Good?" he asked as he straightened up.

"Hell." I shook my head. "What was that?"

"Intense, wasn't it?"

I nodded, still breathing hard. "I'm in trouble."

"Why?" he asked.

"Because I think the risk made it hotter."

He laughed. "Of course it did."

I grabbed him by the shirt, dragging him closer so I could kiss him.

"Not good for a prince. Now I'm going to be thinking about it the rest of the day."

"Good."

"No, not good."

"Yes, good," he said into my lips. "I want you thinking about fucking me all the time."

"But not in public."

"Yes in public. Nothing wrong with a quickie here and there."

I closed my eyes and laid my head back against the door. Yes bad, when this dream couldn't ever be my life. I had to accept it right as I found what may be the perfect man for me, and the realisation might crush me.

XAVIER

It was a new kind of pain to watch Louis from what was probably less than two hundred yards away, in this fucking hotel room, and yet feel so far. He came out to the balcony and stared in the general direction I told him I was in. He was shirtless, probably for my benefit, and had his phone in his hand. He looked up as he typed and then leaned on his forearms on the rail.

My phone buzzed seconds later, and his eyes again looked out in my direction. What was he thinking? I looked at the message.

Louis: I'm thinking about your cock.

Louis: More specifically, I've been thinking about the bathroom incident for days.

No fucking wonder he was looking at me.

X: Have I told you how much I like your filthy mouth?

I could just imagine the look on his face. I picked up my camera and strolled out to my balcony at the higher vantage point. I took just a few pictures of him standing there in all his shirtless glory. Eran would enjoy them. He could make whatever assumptions he wanted on who Louis was texting.

Louis: Is it helping pass the time?

I was about to reply when another text came through.

Louis: If I jack off out here, how many papers do you think it would be the cover of?

I growled. After all I'd done to protect his ass.

X: Are you fucking kidding me?

Louis: You wouldn't publish the photos.

X: No, but we don't know who else can see your damn balcony.

I was seething. He wasn't that stupid.

Louis: You sure do get worked up easily.

Louis: Do you not like the idea of the entire world seeing my cock?

I scrubbed a hand over my face and took a shot of him which I could of course tell he was hard, even from the distance. I took a shot of the screen of my camera with my phone and sent it over.

X: How about this on the cover.

He turned, and I could tell he was adjusting himself.

X: There is an exhibitionist somewhere inside you, isn't there?

Louis: I blame you.

X: If only I could indulge those urges.

Louis: Do you like the idea of fucking me in public?

X: I wanted to fuck you at the club, does that answer your question?

Louis: Bathrooms offer some privacy.

X: I wasn't talking about the bathroom. I meant on the main floor.

Louis dropped his head to his arms and looked like he was struggling to breathe. I picked up my camera to look at him through the telephoto lens. The expression on his face alone when he picked up his head gave me a hard on.

Louis: If only.

And it would end there, but it was fun to banter about.

X: Or up against the window in your suite.

Now he was just glaring at me.

X: You look a little uncomfortable.

Louis: You're getting punished later.

X: Am I? How?

Louis: That would be telling.

I stroked over myself and decided to really mess with him. I yanked down the front of my sweats and took myself in hand getting a shot of my cock. I sent it over without a message figuring it would speak for itself.

Louis: So you're trying to make sure I'm hard on the cover of every magazine?

X: I couldn't help myself.

I pictured the lust in his eyes and how he would touch himself thinking of what I'd done. My phone was buzzing as I stroked up over my length. I'd never done anything like this on a job, but this was different. I was sleeping with the job.

I looked up before I checked my phone, and he was gone. And I saw why when I opened the picture. It was of his hand on his cock.

X: I want to see you stroke it.

I got a short video of his hand moving over himself, and I

watched it three or four times, my mouth watering before I could even gather my thoughts to reply.

X: I want to watch you jack off.

He replied with a longer video. He really was an exhibitionist. I rewarded him with a video of my hand twisting over my cock, precum pooling at my slit.

Instead of his dick, in return I got a video of his face. It was awash in pleasure and he was moaning. It made me hotter than his dick. I was screwed when it came to him. I didn't send another video, I hit the video chat and he answered with a lust filled smile on his face.

"Couldn't wait," he said in a moan.

"No. And I'm doing this on the balcony in full view."

He bit down on his lip groaning. "Good." He flipped the view of the camera to show his cock he was stroking over. He'd stripped down and laid back on the bed, cock at full attention. He played, varying his hand movement from quick to softer. I watched, unable to tear my eyes away as I did the same. It was better than porn.

"Let me see your cock," he demanded.

"I like when you're bossy."

"You don't know how bad I want you in my bed and at my mercy." The way his words rolled off his tongue in his accent nearly had me coming.

"At your mercy?"

"You've had me at yours, and I want you face down with your arse in the air for my pleasure."

I had to hold back my release in gasps. Dark pleasure twisted inside me. "I want to watch your face as you come."

He flipped the camera back around and gave me a wicked

smile. "Naughty."

"I like to see what I do to you." And I did. It was more alluring than even watching him stroke himself, which I planned on making him do later anyway.

He put on a show, and it might have been for my benefit, but I wanted all of it. He moaned and stared into my eyes, bringing himself close to his release. A little crease formed between his dark brows, and I could tell he was concentrating. Every new thing he did sent a rush through my body and turned me on.

"You better be stroking yourself."

I hadn't been, too distracted by what he was doing, but I resumed. "I am," I said totally innocently.

"Liar."

"How quick to judge."

"You forget I can see you." He looked dead on at me, like he could see inside me. "I'm going to punish you for that."

"I can't wait," I said, giving him a wry smile.

"Grab your balls," he ordered. "Pull on them."

I did, groaning. "Like ordering me around, do you?"

He nodded.

"I like when you dirty talk to me. It sounds so sexy in your accent."

"Because it's sophisticated filth." His grin was back.

"When you grin like that I want to shove my cock between your lips."

He slowly licked over them, taunting me. "I'm going to make sure that happens." His breathing started to hitch so I didn't press. I watched as he came, pleasure written on his face and I followed soon after. It wasn't even awkward chatting afterwards, cum spilled over both of us.

"I think that just made my horniness worse."

"Well hurry up and finish so I can taste you in person." The looks he gave me. They bypassed my brain and went right to my cock.

I growled, my chest heaving between lust and frustration at having to sit here. "It could be weeks before he's fucking satisfied."

"Then we'll just have to work something out to get you out of it."

"Does the prince have a plan?"

XAVIER

Two nights later I sat waiting for the action to get started. It wasn't really a big deal, but we figured something was better than nothing if he wasn't willing to use a decoy female, even though both Doug and his sister tried to talk him into it. Even his social secretary said it would be good for his image. She didn't know he was gay, but she did mention when she overheard Doug talking about it, that it had been quite some time since he'd been photographed with a woman, but Louis had told her the agreement he had with his grandmother all over the papers was true, and he said he didn't want anything here to taint a new relationship he started after the summer. How could anyone argue with that?

So here I sat, watching as the hotel room started to fill. It wasn't a large group. Maybe fifteen. Mostly his sister's friends, as he didn't know a lot of people in the area. It was all fine, and I was on board until he told me Drake would be showing his face. The idea of Drake anywhere near him made me blink rage. Every time I saw the dick's face in my mind, my hands curled into fists. I'd never even hit anyone, but I wanted to hit that tool.

Louis had a good argument for inviting him, but it didn't help.

"He's an old friend, and it will look like a set up if one of the only people I know in the area isn't invited. Plus, my sister is inviting a lot of the people he hangs out with. The last thing I need to do is jilt him after his advance," he'd said. "And if he tries something again, I'll tell him I haven't had time to think about it."

I wasn't sure why it was bothering me. It shouldn't have, and yet the hammering in my ears as I waited for him to show wouldn't stop. Louis was leaving. This was stupid. I should have better control of my emotions. I was going to cut things off for good. He was also going to be sleeping with a woman, but for some reason that I didn't quite understand, women didn't bother me as much. Maybe I needed to be evaluated.

So here I was, sitting and watching all of this develop. I wasn't brooding at all. I couldn't even drink like Louis was. Well, a beer, but not the vodka I wanted to be downing while stuck up here with my eyes glued to where I wanted to be.

"Get it the fuck together." I wasn't sure what was going on with me. I was more comfortable out of relationships. I tended to like my own space and solitude, so wanting to be over there was really fucking with me.

Louis walked outside and looked out towards where he knew I was. Like he could meet my eyes. I was sitting in the dark, so where as I might have been visible to him when we'd been sexting, I wouldn't be now.

Anne and the friend she'd been with stepped out on the balcony with him. The friend slid a hand over his arm and around his back. Maybe that was Anne's design with bringing the friend around, although she knew he was gay, and to push that on him…

I shook my head. I needed to stop trying to make sense out of chaos. I needed to sit back and let it be. Not get attached. I'd already got too much invested in this.

Time moved in slow motion, in pictures and images. I was on the outside looking in, and this was my place. My moments pulsed with their music. It wasn't loud, but the wind carried it over to me.

This would be enough for a spread. Eran would be happy. Not to let me off right away, but after a few more quiet nights he would. And then Louis and I could have the rest of our time. There wasn't much of it, but I was going keep it close to my chest and get as much out of this fling as I could.

I was just about to call it a night and go climb in the giant bed I'd have to myself when a light came on in Anne's room. It was a low light, further inside. So I snapped a picture, and then another. She wasn't doing anything but walking around. She'd probably start undressing soon, and I hope she'd pull the curtains. Because those were not the photos I wanted to end tonight with. I wouldn't take them. I would never be that kind of photog, but someone else would. There was no way I was the only one watching this suite. If Eran got a tip, so did others.

She wasn't that stupid. She knew better. She'd spent her entire life being watched. It was one thing to be nude on a private island thinking no one would see you, but this. I shook it off, pushing down my panic. I started to pack up my stuff.

She'd close the curtain and I'd go to bed. I looked at the balcony to see if Louis was still entertaining, but his lights had gone dark. People had left. There would be plenty of suspicion of his company after the party, and there were enough pictures of him close to people to support it. His image would be upheld, and I was happy for him.

I glanced back at Anne's room and nearly dropped my camera. My mouth fell open, and I was digging in my pocket desperately. Where the hell was my phone? Fuck. I brought my camera to my face and took a photo, and then tossed it aside to call Louis. He was not going to be happy.

LOUIS

My phone was ringing. I must have forgotten to put it on silent. I picked it up to flip it on sleep mode when I saw who was calling.

Xavier. He never called.

We were a texting only thing. So I answered it.

"Miss me that much?"

"Check your messages." He sounded grave.

I hadn't done anything wrong. What could there possibly be a picture of? Unless they'd gotten one of he and I. My heart stopped in my chest as I put him on speaker and opened up my messages.

"What is it?"

"Just look." He was so damn tight lipped, and it would have pissed me off if I had to wait any longer to see.

It was nothing I ever expected. I scrubbed a hand over my face and stared.

"I have it, and I'm sure everyone else has it. I wouldn't

send it in, but it will look suspicions if I don't because he is paying for this room."

"You don't have to justify your job to me, Xavier. I understand, and you're right. If you don't send it and your boss sees it elsewhere..." I sighed. I was profoundly sad. She knew better. She fucking knew better. But I'd been seen on the balcony with Xavier, so I had no room to talk.

"If it were anything else I wouldn't send it in. It's trash."

"I have to go talk to her."

"I understand. If I can do anything." The words hung between us.

"Thank you for warning me." I hung up the phone, because he was so good, and it killed me to think he was feeling guilty about it. He'd told us. He'd done the best he could, and I should have told her, but I just wasn't expecting it.

Moments later Anne was answering her door, pulling at her clothes, a half smile on her lips. She was alight with life, and I was going to snatch it from her and it was like a knife to the chest.

"What do you want?"

I held up the picture Xavier had sent me, and she gasped, her gaze flashing to the windows. Tears welled up in her eyes, and she covered her mouth with her hand.

"I'm sorry. I'm so sorry. I wasn't thinking." She looked like she was going to lose it. "I'm so careful. The windows? They are watching me through my own damn windows?" Tears were streaming down her face. Her mascara started to run.

Why hadn't I warned her? I'd completely forgotten.

"Can we get the curtains closed and talk about his?"

She nodded unable to get words out, but she stepped aside.

Her friend was inside half undressed, sitting on the sofa looking confused. I went to the windows and closed them, checking everything, and when I turned back around Anne was wrapping a blanket around her friend.

I held out a hand. "Louis. What was your name again?"

"Jaz," she said, looking between us.

"I'm really sorry to do this to you, but you're going to become quite the news story tomorrow morning."

Her eyes went wide, and she looked to Anne.

"Someone is taking pictures through the window." She'd gotten better control of herself, but tears still streamed down her face.

Jaz's breath hitched, and she looked between us and then down at herself. "Like this?" She was frantic.

I nodded. "I cannot apologise more. These people are ruthless. I wish I could say it horrifies me, but it's not surprising. I wish we could do more for you."

"But. But. But." She was clearly having a hard time processing.

"If there is anyone these pictures will upset you should call them tonight. Like parents?"

She nodded, visibly shaking.

"If you stay out of the public eye, it will die down pretty fast. Again, I apologise."

"I don't give a fuck what they say about me."

"You don't?" I asked

"Fuck no. But the Queen, Anne." There was so much pain in her eyes. She wrapped an arm around Anne and pulled her close. "I swear to god if she says one bad word to you I will go off."

My heart was starting to warm ever so slightly. I liked her already. This girl was going to be exposed publicly, and she cared more about how it would affect my sister than herself. I wanted to hug her.

Anne laid her head on Jaz's shoulder. "It will be fine."

"It will be. I promise." She stroked her finger through Anne's hair.

"I'm going to make some calls," I said. "It's almost morning in London anyway, and the Queen will want to know right away."

Jaz met my eyes as if daring me to reprimand Anne.

"Take care of her, okay?"

She still looked leery, but she nodded, and I backed out of the room.

XAVIER

My picture broke first, but I was right, I was not the only one who had it. I told Eran I wasn't going to sit in the hotel anymore. First off, this wasn't what I wanted to be doing. I wasn't that guy, and secondly, I told him they'd be stupid to let anything else show through the window. Thankfully he agreed with me.

So I was pacing my hotel room watching the TV coverage, waiting for Louis to reply to me. I'd texted him the night before, but he still hadn't responded. I was starting to feel like the pathetic side piece, and I really needed to get my head out of it. Or maybe he was just done with me, after Anne being found out and plastered all over the news, the last thing he needed was for us to be sneaking around.

And I needed to run. I couldn't have my face splashed all over the news. The thought made me lightheaded, and I had to sit down to breathe through it.

It would also put my entire reputation with Eran in

jeopardy, and he'd want pictures. Which I had, but I was never giving anyone. I wanted to get out of this city. I wanted to go back to Chicago and forget about all of this. I picked up my phone trying to figure out what to tell Eran when it started ringing in my hand. Maybe he was going to fire me. Doubtful after the picture I got, but I could dream.

Louis didn't text me back, and by the early afternoon I was pretty sure he was going to avoid me. We'd already cut it too close and now with Anne being caught, he had to be the vision of perfection. I didn't blame him for pushing me away. He had so much to lose, now if only I could get over it.

His smartest move would be to put as much space between us as possible, and a clean break was the only way to do it. If we were back in the same room we'd fuck, and if he called? What an awkward phone call that would be.

By the next morning I was a mess. This was worse than watching him from a distance. This was complete ghost. I was dead. My mind wanted to create a fantasy where this was better for me. I was scared and unfit to exist in my own story. I couldn't imagine being in front of a camera, being stalked, have my picture on the front page of papers, and my scars for everyone to see. I had a hard enough time looking at myself in a mirror, let alone being King Consort. I didn't want to be at his side in public. I only wanted him in private, and he needed more even if he was out.

I was the beast soon to be replaced by a princess.

They say the best way to get over someone was to get under someone else, but I just couldn't bring myself to do it.

Noon came and went. Usually I'd at least get a text, even

if he was preoccupied. My pride wouldn't allow me to text him again. If he was done, the least I could do was let him go in peace.

Showing up for pictures was going to be awkward as hell, but what else could I do? Tell Eran I was done when things had just started to heat up with Anne? He'd want constant photos of her to run. People were interested in the story, so it didn't matter if they were the same photos over and over with outfit changes, there would be clicks.

It was time to get over myself and do my job. I prepped my cameras and checked my email for details on what Eran wanted. There was a short list, and after a little research and reaching out to a few personal assistants, I got some locations to scout out.

As I was walking out the door, my phone started to ring, and I prayed it wasn't something else. I couldn't take any more news about the damn royals. Expecting it to be Eran, I answered.

"Hello?"

"I'm finishing up here and on my way back, could you meet me?" Louis's voice was strained. I could tell he was trying to sound professional. He must be around people.

"Are you intentionally being vague?"

"Yes."

"So you're not avoiding me?" I asked, unsure I even wanted to see him again after being ignored.

"I had some conflicts to attend with. I hope you accept my sincerest apology for not being able to fit you in sooner."

He must really be with people he couldn't speak around. "I didn't deserve a text?"

"I didn't handle things as well as I could have due to the stress of the situation. My attention was elsewhere, and it wouldn't have been fair to you." Just like that, all the panic fled and with the sound of his voice he lured me in.

"Anne needed you."

"Among other things. I can brief you at your earliest convenience."

"Are you asking me over?" Well this was unusual. It was still early.

"Correct."

I was trying not to smile too much or let it come through my voice. "Now?"

"I have a free block in about thirty. I could fit you in."

"You're really trying to be discreet, aren't you?"

"I am."

"So I could have some fun with this?" I laughed.

"I'm sure you could."

"I'll come over, but only if you suck my cock. Hopefully I'm not on speaker."

He groaned. "I'm sure we can discuss such matters in our...meeting."

"Is that what the kids are calling it nowadays? I thought it was Netflix and chill."

He started to growl but cut himself off and turned it into clearing his throat. "What would you like me to call it?" he said in half a whisper.

"A good fuck? It sounds filthy in your accent."

He exhaled audibly. "The arrangements work in my favor, and we'll discuss the details in person."

"Maybe I want to discuss it now. In great detail," I pushed, thinking of him uncomfortable in public.

"I have another call I need to make. Does the meeting work with your schedule?" There was pleading in his tone.

"So disappointing. I guess I'll have to skip leaving marks all over your body if you can't ask for them."

"I don't think you should take such things off the table."

"Getting harder to word isn't it? Maybe I should tell you to beg for my cock."

I was imagining him half hard and pulling at the collar of his shirt.

"If only." It was enough of a break from formal speak to know I'd gotten to him.

"I'm going to leave bite marks just under your collar so you'll think about them every time you shift, hoping it doesn't slip."

A strangled groan was his only reply.

"And then I want your lips around my cock. I'll be sure to give you a good performance review. Since we have to keep this business sounding."

"A review you say?"

"Yes, you're going to need top marks to pass."

"Right then." He sounded entirely uncomfortable, and I loved it.

"I'm waiting for you to say cheerio."

He sighed, and I pictured him pinching the bridge of his nose. "In thirty then?" There was need laced in his words.

"I'll be there and naked, freaking Doug out."

He hung up on me.

Doug was waiting by the time I made it to the back of the

hotel. He grunted at me as I gave him a nod. He checked to make sure there was no one else paying attention before he let me in. We couldn't be too careful, and I was sure at this point he was a well-known face to the staff.

We took a service elevator. Again I wasn't surprised by all the extra precautions. I also wondered how the palace would handle the scandal. I hoped they'd tell the media it was none of their business who the princess fucked, but I doubted that would be the case. They were always so far behind.

Louis wasn't in the room when we got there, and Doug grunted about him being there shortly before he escaped to his room. I looked around the suite. He was here for another two days, and then we'd move again, but it was less than two weeks and he'd be gone, and I'd become the friend. Sometimes I wanted to kick myself.

I needed a drink. I looked around for the bar and wondered if it was indeed too early to start drinking. It probably was. I lingered there with my scotch in hand.

"I thought you were going to be naked," came Louis' smooth accent from behind me. But it was strained, even when he was trying to keep it light.

I put a smile on my face, forcing all the concern out of my head and turned. "You didn't sound too enthusiastic about that on the phone."

He gave me a look. "You know why."

"Am I too filthy for you?" I asked him as I took a step towards him.

"Hardly. I could use more filth in my life." He looked around the room like he was expecting for there to be some window open, some way for us to get caught as I got closer to him.

"Put it all out of your head."

"Easier said than done." But he didn't reject me when I took him in my arms. He leaned into me, and fuck I was screwed when it came to him.

I slipped a hand down his back and started to pull out the back of his dress shirt. He'd already lost the suit coat. He slid his arms around my neck and leaned into me. This wasn't sexual, it was vulnerable and unexpected. I wasn't sure what to say or do. I stood half frozen.

He didn't seem to notice my hesitation.

"Both royals gay?" He pressed his face into my shoulder.

I was shocked, and it took me a moment to catch up. I expected sex and need after two days, but what I got was so much sexier, and at the same time it ripped me apart. He was opening up, being vulnerable. I slid my fingers into his hair, trying to give him as much comfort as I could, but I felt like the meme where the guy is patting the puking girl with a broom saying there there. This was just not something that came naturally to me. I wasn't good with the people or the emotions.

"How did that even happen?" he went on. "Like the odds have to be astronomical."

"Inbreeding?"

He picked up his head and glared. I laughed. I was awkward, and it probably wasn't the best time to lighten the mood, but this was who I was.

"More and more people feel comfortable coming out now, and you did say she said she was bi. A ton of young people are bi, and it's not because this is the gayest generation ever, it's because people have always been bi but they couldn't act on it before." Even as I said it, something was solidifying in my mind. He couldn't be out and gay as King. This would make his choice for him. Because if they forced him out he had even more reason to want to protect Anne. And I could see it. I couldn't even blame him.

"You're probably right, and I know I have absolutely no reason to complain about my life, but why do I have to carry this burden?"

"Just because you're rich and privileged doesn't mean your life is going to be perfect, and no one expects that. Yes, there are plenty of people with it worse off, but you're allowed to be unhappy with your situation."

He pressed his face back into my shoulder, and I played with his hair. "You know, we don't have to stop being friends when you go back." The words burned my mouth as they crossed my tongue, and I knew I'd grow to regret them, but I wouldn't regret the friendship. I'd just regret not getting to go to bed and wake up with him.

He led me toward the bed, stripped me silently, and I allowed him. When we were tucked in he spoke again.

"Do you think we can be friends?" He tugged at my hip, urging my body to roll towards him.

We laid side by side looking into one another's eyes.

"I think so." I swallowed back my feelings. "You need a friend, especially if you're going to pretend to be straight." My words were fucking poison. I wanted to scream at him to come out, to shove his gayness down Parliament's throat. To make them accept him because he was perfect as he was, but I couldn't. I couldn't put that pressure on him. I would have to bury my feelings. I pressed my eyes closed.

"What's wrong?" he asked, placing his palm on the side of my neck.

I couldn't answer right away. I had to bury the words in my soul and lock them away. They were feelings I didn't think I had, but laying here with him, they hit me like a tsunami, and I was going to drown if I let myself feel them.

"Xavier?" he asked, rubbing his thumb over the stubble on my jaw.

"Nothing is wrong. I hate that you have to do this for your country, and there isn't a damn thing I can do about it. So yes I want to be your friend, because it's all I can do." I opened my eyes so I could gauge his reaction and see if he bought my lie.

"I don't deserve you."

"Says the guy giving up love for his country. I don't think so, but you deserve people in your corner."

"Be prepared for texts all hours of the day and night," he said into my lips.

I parted my lips over his lower lip to suck it into my mouth. "Please, you won't have that kind of time." I needed to get as much of him as possible until he left. Maybe it would last me a lifetime if I got drunk enough on his taste.

LOUIS

Our weeks dwindled down to days and then one. We were out of time, and it wasn't enough. I was leaving tomorrow. I'd created this situation, and I still hadn't figured out how I was going to let go. There had to be a way to detach, but it felt like this was the beginning not the end. We were just getting to the good part.

He was coming over for dinner and the night and then tomorrow. I closed my eyes as I stood at my closet. If only I had a choice in this. If only I had a damn choice in my life. But it had been decided long before I was born. I was living a life where everything had been set in motion, and I barely got to decide what I ate. Even my clothes were decided for me for most events, run though nineteen people before they got to me.

There was a knock on my door. I looked at my watch. I wasn't even dressed. Not that it mattered. We seldom wore clothes anymore when we were together, but I did want to look nice. Doug had helped me find a nice little place to have catered in, and well this was something.

The lock clicked, and the door opened. Doug looked at me in just my boxers and then held a hand over his eyes. "Your guest. I guess I'll go personally wait for your dinner because it gets me out of this room."

"He seems more like a butler of late than a security guard."

"He's pretty much anything he wants to be."

Xavier started to loosen his tie as he approached. I put my hand over his to stop him.

"You want to keep me clothed? How selfish."

"Maybe I like looking at you all dressed up."

"Strange isn't it?"

It was strange, but sexy and distinguished. He really pulled it off. "Maybe you should do it more often."

"Makes me feel weird." He tugged on his tie again.

I put my hand over his as I leaned in to kiss him. "Let me have this, please."

He looked into my eyes and nodded, dropping his hand. "Did you switch to cocoa butter?" He learned in closer, acting like he was sniffing my neck but brushed his lips over my jaw. "Cocoa butter with cinnamon. I would know it anywhere. Did Doug make a trip to Lush?"

"Please, if I wanted to go to Lush I'd go myself."

I could feel his smile against my skin. "Then what would the papers say?"

"That I'm supporting a British company."

"I'm buying you gold bath bombs."

His words put images in my head. Probably the opposite of what he was intending, but they were there all the same. I had images of him and I held up in a hotel. I had nowhere to be. I would just return to my drinking and being miserable between events the social secretary chose for me. I had a lot of ideas about starting charities for queer kids, but first I would need to hide and lick my wounds. I'd never been through a break up, and this one was going to be a doozy. I could already feel it coming on, and I didn't want to be that guy, but I was that guy.

"Not even a laugh. You're really getting bath bombs for your birthday. Which I googled by the way. So I know when it is. I've never dat... Been with a guy I could google details about."

"Don't believe everything you read." I slipped a hand around his back, but I was stuck in my fantasy.

"Like that you're a womanizer?"

I pressed my lips to his. "Most of it is made up."

"I can tell. For one, they have no idea what a board game nerd you are." He parted his lips and stroked his tongue over the seam of mine.

"A sexy nerd?"

"Totally."

I parted my lips for him and was consumed by the kiss.

"Let me get dressed." I pressed my forehead to his and took him in.

"You should definitely not get dressed." His hand moved to my arse.

"You know Doug is coming back with dinner."

"You can eat naked. I'm sure Doug's seen that plenty of times."

"I'd prefer not to sexually harass my employees." I made myself step back from him. If I kept close for another minute

I might beg him to stay. Forever.

"That's fair, but isn't part of his job keeping watch while you were having one night stands?"

"He didn't keep watch."

"Maybe he likes watching." Xavier laughed and wiggled his brows. "Don't judge him."

"He was only in charge of frisking them, which I'm sure is a kink of his from the enjoyment he seems to get out of it, and escorting them out."

"So sterile. But at least he was nice to me." Xavier fixed his clothes. "I don't think I could wear these all the time."

"No?" I asked, imagining a world where he was allowed to be by my side and would have to wear clothes like those. Maybe I shouldn't ask him. There was a good chance he would never want anything of the sort. He wasn't the type to seek out a prince.

I dressed, and he watched, his eyes lingering on my body. I wondered what he was here for. It couldn't be hard for him to hook up, and yet here he was playing by my rules. Left in bed while I went to be in the public. Being a secret. Did it weigh on him as much as it did on my soul?

There was a knock on the door, and Doug slipped in. "Got a few questions about the amount of food, since Anne is visibly out tonight."

"They are dogs. They really looked at how much food we ordered?"

"I think everyone wants to assume you're here with someone," Xavier commented. He took the bags from Doug and started to set out boxes on the table.

"You can have the night off, Doug. We won't be going

out."

He looked between the two of us and nodded before making his exit.

"I'm shocked he feels safe enough to leave me alone here with you."

I laughed. "You're mostly harmless."

He cocked his head and looked at me. "Are you making sneaky book references?"

I lifted a shoulder. "Would you believe that I take books with me while I indulge in bath bombs?"

"I'm imaging a bathroom all in gold and white marble as big as my loft. There's a string quartet positioned in the corner, playing soothing music, and a butler. I'm imagining Doug in a suit, bringing you over champagne and strawberries on a silver tray, along with a selection of books for you to choose from."

I laughed so hard tears came to my eyes. "How did you get through that entire scene with a straight face?"

He flashed me a grin. "Talent."

"I don't know what's more ridiculous." I shook my head. "The string quartet in the corner was a nice touch."

"Act like you're not thinking about how they would enhance future baths."

I scrubbed a hand over my face as I made myself a plate. "I'm imagining what the papers would say. We'd have a Marie Antoinette scene on our hands."

He sat next to me instead of at the far end of the table. It was so insignificant, but it meant the world to me. "I'd miss your head if it was detached from your body."

"How elegant of you to word it." I stood having forgotten

drinks. "Do you want something?"

"Can you get me a soda water, honey?" He laughed and then went on, "This is so domestic of us. I don't think I can handle it."

I set the drinks down and looked at him. "Should I light candles?"

He offered me what looked like a forced smile, and I couldn't tell why because he deflected it with more jokes. "Is the prince trying to get lucky?"

"Isn't he always?" I asked.

He pointed at me with his fork. "Too true."

There was profound sadness in his eyes, and I was starting to believe it mirrored what was in my heart.

"What are you thinking?" I paused and then added. "Really thinking. No jokes or deflections this time."

He shook his head. "I can't." His eyes pressed closed, and he took a pained breath.

I put my hand over his, scooting closer to him. "Please talk to me."

"If I talk it will make it too real."

I slid off my chair, coming to rest on my knees next to him. "This is more than superficial, and we are going to regret it if we don't talk about it."

"We have a fucking expiration date, and it's tomorrow and we're both trying to act like it's not choking off everything, but it is. And I know I agreed to this day, but I like you, I really fucking like you, and I'm sorry if I'm struggling but this is hard. Sitting here pretending not to be dreading the movement of the sun, cursing every minute that passes is rough. I'm trying to put on a face for you because I really do think you need to have a friend after this, but I want to flip tables and destroy this hotel room." He pushed his plate back and pressed his forehead into the table. It was shockingly dramatic for him, and I finally felt like I was getting the real emotions not masked with humour.

"It's killing me too." I had nothing to offer but my solace.

He turned his head and looked over at me. "I think that's part of it. Part of me feels that from you, but there is another part of it that sees your calm and collected exterior and thinks this is just another day in your life. You're so closed off to feelings because you have to be, and that's fine, I can't even imagine what your life must be like, but to not have my feelings returned." He shook his head.

I came to kneel between his knees and took his face in my hands. "The feelings are returned. I know we talked about the time limit, and this coming to an end, but what if we had one more weekend?" I knew I was crazy. The idea was crazy, but I had some downtime coming after this tour. I could spend it as I wished, and if we went into hiding we could pull it off.

"Do you really think prolonging the goodbye will make it any better?"

"I don't know. All I know is I'm not ready to let you go yet."

He looked skeptical. "What do you mean?"

I was putting myself out there. I was being reckless, and I just couldn't bring myself to care. I had justified it to myself and I deserved it. He didn't feel the way I did, and it was fine, but I wanted one selfish weekend to hold on to for the rest of my life.

"Come to London."

XAVIER

I'd had reservations about the entire thing, but here I was on the massive Airbus with an entire stateroom to ourselves. I was hiding in plain sight with him. He didn't want most of his staff to know, so I'd been smuggled aboard, and by smuggled I mean I showed up hours before schedule with Doug, when there was hardly anyone at the private airport. While Louis arrived hours later with the rest of his escort.

I took the time to explore, trying to imagine the indulgence of owning a private jet, but I lacked the capacity.

Louis took a seat in one of the posh chairs and kicked his feet up. He looked tired. I didn't blame him. I was tired looking at his schedule. I stayed where I was with my drawing pad on the far side of the room. I flipped to a new page and started to sketch his outline. I wondered if he'd let me publish the pictures and drawings after his death. If I outlived him that was. It would be a shame for the world not to see this side of him.

"You look deep in thought."

I looked up from the paper. "You looked like you needed few minutes to decompress."

He nodded staring out the window. "I can't believe it's over."

"I thought you didn't want to be here?"

"You changed that." He shifted to face me. "What are you thinking about?"

"The differences in our lives."

He nodded somberly. It clearly depressed him. It was a shocking realization. Money didn't prevent problems. Money made your problems different, but they still existed. Don't get me wrong, I'd still rather be rich, and there were still people who couldn't put food on the table, so more money was life and death to them. It was all about perspective.

"And now you look deep in thought."

"I was thinking of all the things that you have to go back to and why you can't disqualify yourself." It was starting to solidify in my mind then. There was so much he needed to do, and maybe if we stayed friends I could keep pushing him towards those things.

"You've changed your mind?" He took a seat in the chair across from me. "What happened?"

"I've done a lot of introspective thinking. I think a gay king would be great. I think if you came out it would show a lot of people identity is more important than money or titles, but I know why you won't, so I know what you need to do."

"What do I need to do?" He leaned forward, resting his elbows on his knees.

"You need to do more. More for LGBT people. More for

poor people. More opportunities for lower class to get to the middle class."

A smile tugged at the corner of his mouth.

"What?"

"I'd ask you to stay and help me with those things, but I'm not sure we could be trusted to be in such close proximity."

I exhaled roughly. I wanted to laugh, but he was probably right. "I'll have to help from across the globe."

"Will you actually?"

"Maybe." The idea of being friends with him was still too raw. And I needed to change the subject. "So what are we going to do on this long ass flight?" I leered at him, giving him my best bedroom eyes.

The door banged open, and Anne waltzed in. "I knew there was something juicy going on in here." She batted her eyelashes and smirked at both of us. "When my brother said he had a headache and was going to 'lay down'." She made air quotes as she said it. "So we are smuggling home a sex slave then?"

I nodded my head. "At your service. The sex slave."

She wiggled her finger at me and looked at Louis. "He's cute."

Louis smiled and nodded. "My apologies, I should have introduced the two of you sooner."

She waved him off. "I understand wanting to keep the toy to yourself, but we have six fucking hours on this plane, and I'm bored. So before you two get to play you have to entertain me."

"Damn, and here I was hoping to join the mile high club."

Louis' gaze shifted towards me as he drew in a sharp

breath.

I lifted my shoulder and gave him a wry smile. "Like you've never thought about it."

"On the royal plane, no less. Dirty, I need to do that." Anne's eyes were alight.

"You two talk about a lot, don't you?" I asked as she came over and claimed the sofa across from us and set down the box she was carrying.

"A lot."

"Except I didn't know you are a lesbian."

She rolled her eyes. "Pansexual. I don't care what's in the trousers. I care about personality, and the rest is a pleasant surprise."

"Do you want to have this conversation in private?"

She shook her head. "It doesn't bother me. I've thought about coming out for about a year, but after all the other stuff I knew it wasn't the right time. I didn't want the two to get mixed up." She offered a tight smile, and I wondered how much pain was closeted for the sake of a country.

Anne picked one of the games she'd brought in and started to set it out. I came over to look over her shoulder, and she started to explain it to me.

"She doesn't believe in giving passes to novices. You're screwed," Louis said as he took a seat across from Anne. "Start from the beginning. At least give him a chance."

She stuck her tongue out at Louis and then got out the actual directions to go over.

"I'm still confused," I commented after Anne explained the rules for the second time.

"Why don't we just start? You'll get the hang of it

playing."

"She's ruthless, don't believe her," Louis commented as he started to give us pieces.

"Are you speaking from experience of getting your ass kicked?" I asked.

Anne giggled and nodded. "He is."

"I win…"

"Occasionally," Anne finished for him. "When luck looks upon you."

Anne handed me the directions before we started. "For reference." Then she patted my hand like I was a dotard.

After about twenty minutes of playing, I realized I was in over my head. Not only was there a load of strategy involved in the game, but an entire set of rules and points to keep track of.

"Is this the secret way they train you guys to conquer the world?" I asked, scrubbing a hand over my face as I tried to grasp for the ends of what was going on in the game.

Anne's mouth twisted up in the corners. "Innocent on the outside, but it makes us ruthless."

"As long as you're not terrorizing the world anymore, I guess. You royals are blood thirsty."

"It's a game."

"Must be genetic. At least you're keeping your armies to a board game."

Anne scoffed. "It is a little sad I enjoy this so much."

"From all the inbreeding," I said, looking at Louis.

Louis smacked me. "We have amended our ways."

"As long as your aspirations when you're king don't involve conquering in more than board games."

"You know very well they don't."

"I'm not so sure after seeing the ruthless way your sister plays board games."

Louis leaned over and brushed his lips over mine. "Just another reason she can't have the crown."

"No shit. I'd be scared for the rest of the world."

"Me too."

Anne glared at us both.

I laid my forehead on the table about two-thirds into the game. "I give up."

Anne tisked. "You did fine for your first time. I really did throw you in head first."

"I think all of the people who play these are mentally superior to me."

Louis rubbed a hand down my back. "Everyone is like this their first time."

"Most are worse usually. We tried with our cousins and they couldn't grasp it at all. At least you got the basics."

"She also picked a damn hard beginner game." Louis glared at Anne playfully.

"Probably trying to gauge if I'm worthy."

Anne nodded. "He gets me."

"Do I pass?" I asked.

"With flying colours," she replied.

"Then I guess it was all worth it." I turned to face Louis, and the smile he wore was going to kill me. I fit here, in private, and in public I was the opposite of what they needed. It ripped me open like a serrated knife to my heart.

Anne looked between us. "I'll leave you two to it." She flashed me a wink and bounded out.

"She doesn't seem her age."

"No, she's always been young at heart." Louis moved closer to massage my shoulders.

I moaned. "That feels good."

He started to use both hands and worked his thumbs into my muscles. "Good. I want you to feel good."

"The airplane sex has been brewing in your head hasn't it?"

"There isn't a time I don't want to fuck you," Louis replied.

"Can we talk first?"

His face fell, which I hated, and it was hard not to react.

"Can you not look at me like I'm going to break up with you?"

"But you are, aren't you?"

"It's not me breaking up with you. We aren't even anything." He couldn't be anything with me.

Pain was written in the look he gave me. "No, I guess not."

My fingers dug into the armrests of my seat. "At every step of this I've done want you want. Been as easy as possible for you. Because I know this is hard for you. But it's fucking hard for me too. Can you not assume the worst of me the first time I need to talk about things?"

"I apologise. I should hear you out, but you have such an effect on me. You don't know."

"No, I don't," I muttered.

My chest ached with a wound that hadn't even been ripped open yet. We'd spent so much time trying to keep this casual we'd not even taken the time to tell each other how we felt. Wasted so much time. And now that it was coming to an end it was only going to make things harder if we knew, and I could only assume he wasn't about to open up to be splintered when it ended.

"Please proceed." I could tell Louis was bracing for the worst.

"It wasn't even about us." I turned to look out the window. "We can talk about it later."

"No, I want to hear it." He pulled my chair closer so our knees were intertwined. He reached out to brush his fingers over my cheek. "It's important to me."

I let out a pent up breath and pushed my hands into my hair, still not looking at him. "You know how you said I could help with political direction and charities?"

"Yes."

"Well I thought a lot about it, and well, I think you should embrace Anne's queerness."

Shock crossed his expression.

I reached over to smooth the lines in his brows. "Hear me out."

"I will. I will always listen to you."

I took another deep breath. "It's already out there, and whereas I know you can't do it, she can. She has nothing to lose. The public has already seen it. Why not embrace it and use it to spur the human rights campaign?"

He slipped his hand into mine. "I think I should. I don't know if she'll be comfortable talking about it since she was basically forced out of the closet, but maybe in time she will want to embrace it." He was quiet for some time before he spoke again. "Can we not talk about us until after this weekend? Let me have the weekend. Then I'll talk as much as you want about us, and feelings, but I want to forget with you for a little while."

"That's what you thought I was bringing up?"

He nodded. "I thought you wanted to leave already."

I bit my tongue. There was so much I wanted to say, but I honored what he asked and kept it to myself. What could I say?

I'd stay if he'd asked me right then. It was easier if he didn't know the power he wielded. The power I'd handed over without even realizing it. So I stayed quiet.

He'd be King, and I the pauper.

I'd beg at his feet if it meant continuing the high only he could provide.

If I told him it would ruin us both. I had to be strong for both of us and be the one to let go.

XAVIER

There were no questions after we landed and Louis and I were shuffled into different cars. He was going to the palace, and I was going to the apartment. I'd put on a suit so I'd fit in and it didn't look strange when I walked into the Connaught. I'd googled the place when Louis told me about it, and shit. It was, well, it was posh. There was no other word for it from a guy like me who was used to eating easy mac in his loft. Doug came with me, which I thought was strange, but I'd ignored it. I was sure there was a reason. No one kept track of the employees, except my kind, so we were probably safe. They were following Louis back to the palace. We were ignored. Anne was going to make a big scene tonight to help us out as well, so Louis could get free without anyone noticing.

The interior of the Connaught was everything I'd expected London to be with hand-carved crown molding, frame molding creating a lovely inlaid texture to the walls, exquisitely painted in a cool palette, and trey ceilings with chandeliers. It all had a sense of aristocracy I could never aspire to.

I wanted to put on a hoodie and retreat to my loft. I didn't fit in with people. I was better behind a camera or online. What the fuck was I thinking coming here? More evidence I didn't fit into his life or his world. I was still wondering when Doug came and found me in the bar I'd wandered into. It had a darker aura, contrasting black leather furniture with cream and gray woven into the frame molding. Black vases cracked with gold lines and bright white hydrangeas on the tables. Low lights hung from ornate fixtures. And the bartenders were all in waistcoats with actual pocket watches. I aspired to the level of coolness they displayed at work.

I was starting to suspect everyone in London was given more badass points at birth. I slipped my hands in my pockets as Doug touched my shoulder. I turned on him and he must have seen it in my eyes.

"You never get used to it."

I nodded because I was sure he was right. Hell, how long had he worked for the guy and been in and out of places like this, yet he was still admitting it. Or maybe he was trying to be nice. Either way I appreciated it.

He bypassed the normal elevator and went around to a private elevator with its own private entrance. I sighed but wasn't surprised. It was even more evident when we got to the penthouse why there was a private elevator. The kinds of people who rented The Apartment villa at the Connaught needed the privacy not having to go through the lobby allowed. I wanted to ask who'd rented it last. It was probably Bono or some shit. Big glasses bastard was probably all up in this shit. Good thing they changed the sheets.

The room was lovely, and I didn't have better words for it. I considered myself a well educated guy, but design was not my forte. The room was done in cream and periwinkle accents and I was pretty damn impressed with myself for knowing the color periwinkle. There were even hydrangeas matching the decor.

I sunk to a seat on one of the sofas. It hadn't hit me until now. Sure, the hotels were nice in Canada, but it was Canada. This was another level entirely. What the fuck did Louis see in me? Was he slumming it? Dating the riffraff to get it out of his system? I really wasn't liking how I was feeling about the disparity in our social class. Something I'd never given a thought to before.

It was a horrible dick thing to do, but I wanted to leave before he got here. Cut it off here where it should have been.

LOUIS

Why was it always raining in London? It was a question for the ages, and I breezed through Buckingham Palace dripping wet and not giving a fuck. I was followed by at least two butlers and a maid with hand towels as they tried to both dry me and the floor behind me as I walked. I thought of shaking like a dog but decided if I wanted to sneak away for the weekend I was going to have to be on my best behavior. Responsibility sucked.

The Queen was waiting with tea. Always tea. I was an addict, and basically drank the stuff all day long, but I felt like an extraordinary cliché. A pinky up type of fuck. I took a seat on the cloth someone had laid down before me. The ornate future in here was probably at least twelve generations old, so I didn't really blame them, but it made me miss hotels, or even the idea of Xavier's loft. I bet he wouldn't care if I walked in the door sopping wet and sat on the furniture. He'd probably encourage me to strip down before climbing in his bed, but we weren't animals.

My grandmother wasn't big on speaking first. She liked to play this cat and mouse game, staring at her guests with her one creepy eye that opened slightly more than the other, daring them to be brave enough to speak to her. Most people trembled in fear waiting for her to start a conversation only to be given this look for eight or ten minutes until they started babbling. It was all a power play. I couldn't be bothered with it.

"How's it going?" I asked.

She raised an eyebrow at me. "Did Canada teach you slang?"

"Hardly." I laughed as I doctored up my tea.

"Clearly, it hasn't taught you moderation." She eyed the now mostly empty sugar bowl.

"It's your fault I'm spoiled."

"I should have hired better nannies."

"Do not bring Bridgette into this." I pointed my spoon at her.

She rubbed her temples. "I thought we agreed to no scandals while you were away?"

"I can't help the outrageous actions of the paparazzi shooting through a damn window." I was sticking to the script. It was their behavior not Anne's actions. She did nothing more than nearly every person on the planet in their own space.

"No, but we can try and use things like curtains. It's called common sense, Louis."

"Why are you yelling at me? There aren't any photos of my room," I countered.

She pursed her lips.

"And I'm sure she feels like an idiot, but she's entitled to privacy, and who the hell really expects her to remain a virgin?"

She shrugged, which was as much of an agreement as I was going to get. I wanted to say more. To tell her it would be good for Anne to be out. I wanted to defend my sister and say all the stuff Xavier had told me would be good for the country, but I wasn't ready. I'd made up my mind, but really it was Anne's choice, and I needed to talk to her first before I brought it up to my grandmother.

"It will be good to see how the government reacts."

I cocked my head. "Huh?"

"Is proper English really beyond you? What did I pay tutors for?"

"What do you mean?" I asked, too curious to play her games and return the sarcasm.

"It will be a good measure for the country. I don't know how the papers looked there, but there has been quite a lot of positivity after the initial shock."

I blinked a few times.

"Struck dumb?" she asked.

"A little."

"I think this will spark a good debate across the country. She isn't you. They can't do anything about whom she sleeps with. Not like she's the heir."

No, she wasn't, just another reason I was screwed by birth order. I needed even more to get out of here. Away from duty. Away from bloody everything. I would have a breakdown if I didn't get some time.

"I'm going to take some time to myself. I was gone for two months."

She waved me off. "I expected as much." She looked at me over her tea cup. It was a little scary. "Stay out of the papers."

"Obviously."

She gave me a flat look only a tiny woman with more power than God could give.

"I really mean it to be some time to reflect before we go forward with our deal." I sounded like an idiot, but I didn't want to say too much or too little to make her suspicious.

"You're entitled. I'll expect you back in a week, ready."

The 'ready' looked like it pained her as much as it pained me. "I know."

A weight settled on my shoulders as I walked out of the palace. A weight I didn't want to bring with me for my one week of peace before I had to return to my life, but what other choice did I have? I just hoped Xavier couldn't sense it.

Doug met me at the private entrance. I was wearing a baseball cap, which in itself was strange for me, but I wanted to go as unnoticed as possible. I had this elevator ride to get myself under control and enjoy this. I wanted this. I needed this, all emotions aside, and if I bought my feelings into the room, we'd talk and I'd lose it. I didn't want this weekend to be about how unfair my life was. I wanted a chance to enjoy Xavier without thinking. Now how to do this? How to be with the person I could see myself dating, see myself having something real with. If Doug weren't here I would have wanted to hit something or someone. I'd wished I'd gone to the private gym before coming here. Getting some of this out in the ring would have helped. But here I was, and I had to face him.

LOUIS

Collecting him in my arms when I walked in took away all the pent up pain and anger. I was focused on him and us for the first time in my life, with no other obligations. It was like living an entirely different life. We spent the time learning each other inside and out. We played board games, so badly Anne would have been ashamed, and we marathoned television shows he enjoyed and I'd never had time to watch.

We laid in bed while it rained, and days turned into nights and back to days. I got used to waking up to him drawing and lazy mornings in bed. Something we hadn't been able to enjoy while I was on tour. We ate meals together, and breakfast with him became my favourite part of the day. He seemed to take the queen's side on my sugar intake in the morning and told me I'd be dead by the time I was forty.

It was bliss. A kind of bliss I hadn't known existed. Maybe there was something to running away to a tropical island for a gap year like Drake had. I wanted a gap year from being prince. If only there was a such a thing. In the back of my mind I knew the more time I took the harder ending it would be, but it didn't stop me from extending my time from a weekend to a week and then ten days.

For the first time in my life I wanted to hide away for the rest of my life. I'd give up a Kingdom for him if he'd let me. Was love more important than duty? I was meant to be King, but with him I was me, and maybe I liked the private me more. I liked the me I was with him, and maybe that was worth risking everything for.

I shook my head trying to force out all thoughts of the future. I was going to relish in him. Time was fleeting, and I had to drink in what I could.

"What are you thinking about?" he asked, breaking me out of my head.

I stroked my fingers down his bare skin. "How I never want to leave this hotel."

He chuckled. Probably sure I was joking.

"It's pretty great." He looked around the room. "But it can't have anything on a palace."

As far as luxury went, once a certain level was hit it was all the same. Something I wouldn't utter as I didn't want to sound like an elitist bastard, but the shades of difference were minimal.

"What do you think this is missing that the palace has?" I asked, more curious as to what played through his head than anything else.

"We talked about this. Golden toilets and the string quartet in the bathroom."

I burst out laughing. "Golden loo, that's rich."

"Gold leaf toilet paper then?" he asked.

"Yes, because I want everything left behind. You know what gold leaf does right?"

"Can't say I've ever been rich enough to handle it."

I gave him a flat look. "It's sticky like."

"Does that make your asshole like goldschlager? That's something I could get on board with."

I coughed and kept laughing. "Hell, you've got quite the imagination. Next you'll be saying you're drunk off me."

"If the gold leaf has anything to do with it."

"I see how it is. You just want me for my money." I pulled him closer.

"And to be drunk off of it." He came willingly, and my lips found his in the morning light. "I never through I'd be in London and not want to leave my hotel room."

"Well you never expected it to be as posh as this."

"Or have the company of the future king."

"Please, you fantasized about this all the time."

He looked at me for a moment before a smile broke over his face. "You're right. I was gold hunting for my sugar daddy. The books I'll be able to write when you die."

"Who said I'll die before you?"

"That's the part you take issue with? Not the book or me calling you daddy?"

"If it gets you going you can call me daddy."

He laughed. "Not my thing. And the books?"

"I'll be dead, what will I care? Scandalize the country all you want."

"I'm taking that as a verbal contract."

I scoffed and smacked him lightly. "Arse." This strange

feeling came over me, and for the first time in my life I felt entirely normal. Like I was no different than any other bloke in love.

"You're a little young for my normal, and too public…" but I didn't hear him.

Love resonated through me. I was in love with this guy. My heart ached at the thought of him returning home. At losing him. Not being able to talk to him every day.

"Louis?" and my name on his lips. Could I beg him to stay?

Something in me started to change in that moment.

"I'm here."

"Are you falling asleep? I don't think you heard anything I said." He said it with a smile as he pushed his fingers into my hair.

I turned my head and kissed his palm. "Maybe a little." Or falling into my own thoughts. Something I rarely had the time to consider with as busy as I was.

"How much longer do you think you have before they send out the search party?" he asked.

"At least another day. My grandmother can be patient, and I did tell her I needed some time." It had already been a while, and I'd gotten a few calls.

It was a game of chicken I was going to play as long as possible. Ignore them until they dragged me back and shackled me to the throne.

XAVIER

It was like a dream being here. I could never in my wildest dreams afford this place. It was the definition of posh, and it seemed like nothing to Louis. Compared to a palace it probably was nothing. For a little while I was able to forget reality. I hadn't even checked my email while I'd been here. Everyone probably thought I was dead, and I couldn't bring myself to care.

"What are you thinking about?" he asked from across the breakfast table.

He had a paper open, and it was entirely domestic for him to look over the top of it and ask me what I was thinking.

"What are we, an old married couple?"

His brow scrunched in the middle and then a smile appeared on his lips. "It feels a little like it doesn't it?"

"More than a little." I took a sip of my coffee from the china I could never afford and looked over the spread between us.

"What are you really thinking?" he pressed.

"How I need to stop getting used to this." *Used to him,* I finished in my head.

His phone started to buzz on the table next to him. He picked it up and frowned.

"Who is it?" I asked.

"It's Anne."

"Answer it," I replied.

"I'm not sure I want to."

"It's the third time she's called this morning." We'd been left alone, and I suspected our time was getting strained. Every time Louis extended it to more days, I stayed. I couldn't bear to leave, but how much longer could he hide?

"I know." He stood up and stepped onto the balcony to take the call.

I sat back and laced my fingers behind my head. Him taking the call outside was like a bucket of ice water on our little fantasy. He probably didn't want me to know how bad it was getting. How annoyed the Queen was with him. Neither one of us wanted to be rational.

"I have to go home," he said quietly when he stepped back inside.

I'd known it was coming, and it still gutted me, like he'd ripped my insides out and left them lying on the floor between us.

"Anne says I'm going to be hunted down by the Queen if I don't reappear. She can only cover for me so long."

"It's not like it would be hard to find us. We are basically in your backyard."

"I know." His head hung from his neck like the weight of

it was too much to bear.

I crossed to him and collected him in my arms, but I was at a loss for words. I didn't have words to comfort my damn self, what could I possible offer him?

"Don't leave," he pleaded.

"Even if you go beg for a few more days it's just pushing off the inevitable."

"No—" he stopped and started again. "Don't leave at all. Stay here." He gestured around the apartment. "You like it here. I'll rent the room indefinitely."

"And what? Wait here like a kept boy?"

"You could work here. It'd be like Canada."

I shook my head. "You have an agreement with the Queen."

"We'll work something out. Just don't leave yet." His grip tightened on my arms.

"We have a fucking expiration date, you know that, and I know that, but we have to start acting like it."

"What if I don't want to think about it?"

"You said that ten fucking days ago. And I did what you asked, but we can't just keep pretending."

"But I want to." There was a despair in his eyes I prayed I'd never have to see again. It broke me into tiny irreparable pieces.

"This is the major difference between us. You wanted to pretend the expiration date didn't exist, and I want to hold on to it so I know how important each moment is."

He pushed his fingers into my hair. "I wanted to forget it so I could focus on the moments, because if I focused on the day I had to return to my life it was going to taint everything and I would want to close off."

"Don't close off."

"I'm trying not to." He closed his eyes, and looking into his face was heaven. I tried to memorize the moment. Etching every detail of him and this room into memory. "We wasted so much time in the beginning. Give me a few more days."

"We wasted entirely too much." I turned my head to kiss his palm. "But more time isn't going to make it easier."

"I know." He left the words there like they'd change anything. Or maybe he needed to hold on to infinity to get through this.

I had a life, or at least the idea of one when he left. What did he have? Duty. It was a lonely road, but if I'd learned anything about him, he'd do it just to make sure the burden never fell to anyone else.

I fought back the wave of emotion I was feeling. This was already too hard, and if he asked enough I just might stay and be his side piece, and I couldn't live with myself if I did that. It wasn't right, and it would kill me if he asked me to.

I straightened up, mustering up any bit of composure I could find. "Louis." Just his name on my lips was like a hammer to my heart. I avoided looking at him. "Louis if I agree to stay another week I'll never leave. And if I stay you're going to be married, and I'll have to watch it on TV, then you'll have kids, probably more than one, and I get your dedication. But I can't live with myself being here, staying in this apartment when you have a wife to go home to at night, and I'm not even saying you don't have the best of intentions." I blew out a breath I didn't know I'd been holding. "I am positive you could find a woman who wants to be a princess so bad she'd agree to be your wife only in show. Even in a totally honest relationship where no one is being lied to, I still can't have you at night. I can't spend the very little personal time you'll have with you. I have no life here. No job. I have nothing, and if I do this I know I won't be happy. But more than that, I'm tired of people in power hiding in the closet." I pushed my fingers into my hair. "You mean the world to me, and I understand your reasons, but when you have a platform to make change and you're going to do nothing..." I shook my head. "I just can't be the one who is this for you. I'm sure you'll have no issue finding someone who would be." And I was sick as I said it. Because I knew who would slip right into my position. Drake. He'd already offered, and now that Louis thought he needed this there wasn't any reason for him not to do it.

Louis didn't say a thing. He stood there and stared at me. He swallowed a few times, and maybe I was glad he didn't try and argue. I was on ice, and it was splintering under my feet. One word from him might send me plunging into the depths with no chance of ever coming back up.

I needed to get out of here. I needed to get on a plane back to Chicago and bury myself in work.

"Just stay until I get back."

"Okay," I said as he walked out the door, hating myself for lying to him.

As soon as he walked out of the door I was packing. There was no other way to do it. I couldn't leave while he was here, and the longer I stayed the harder it would be. I had to do it while he was gone, even if he never forgave me. I shoved the clothes back into my suitcase. I'd barely worn any of them since we'd spent most of our time naked and in the robes, which I was stealing. As I packed, I sunk into the memories, trying to keep each and every one. All the places we'd fucked and all the times I'd made him laugh. I could feel his hands on my hips pulling me close as I zipped my suitcase closed.

I wrote him a letter and set it on the bed. I was out the door in under twenty minutes, being sure not to give him enough time to get back and ask me to stay one more time. I knew I wouldn't have the resolve if I had to leave with him watching me.

LOUIS

I walked into her office and she looked me up and down. "Sit," she commanded. Maybe it was because I'd always known her as Queen or because of the years of being who she was, but nothing ever seemed like a request. Her words were demands to be honoured.

I sat in one of the floral print chairs and poured myself a cup of tea. There were no butlers or servants when we had tea. It was an understanding we'd had since I was young. If I told her we needed to have tea it was just us. Just family. She was all I had after all.

She finished up what she was doing at the desk. It still amazed me the pieces of history I was constantly surrounded by, and most of the time took for granted. I'd led a privileged life where privilege came from.

I wanted to make up some other reason to be here. I wanted to lie. All the courage I'd had only the day before fleeing, but his words kept playing over and over in my mind. I ran my fingers over the fabric of the chair. It probably cost more than most people made in a year. There were so many gay kids. Kids who didn't have the luxuries I did. Kids who'd be kicked out that night, kids who'd be beaten to death, kids who would be mocked by their peers until they ended things. It was in my power to help accomplish change. What kind of person would I be if let that pass me by? It would erase all the good I could even accomplish as King.

I was lost in thought when my grandmother came and sat in the seat next to me. She got my attention by pouring herself a cup of tea. She was one of the busiest people on the planet, but she never rushed our time. If I needed it she let me take all I needed, and that simple thing told me I was more important to her than her country, which was saying a lot from a woman who'd lived her whole life for duty.

"Even you aren't quiet this long. You're starting to worry me."

I looked at her, still trying to muster my courage. I pressed my eyes closed. I was going to be such a disappointment. She'd have to go with Anne, whom she never called a disappointment, but she worried about Anne as much as I did, and I just knew that having to put that pressure on Anne would kill her.

"Please don't tell me you knocked up some American." She rubbed her temples. She was mostly joking. I could tell by her tone.

"It might be worse." I didn't mean to say it, but the words slipped out.

She gave me a stern look. "Whatever it might be we will deal with it."

I took a deep breath and nodded. "I'm gay."

She laughed. She fucking laughed. I felt like I was in the twilight zone. Why the hell was she laughing? I was sure the shock showed on my face, because she put her hand on my knee but didn't stop laughing for at least another two full minutes.

I started to look around. "Am I on some damn hidden camera show?"

She wiped her eyes. "I was wondering when you were going to tell me. I really thought all the talk about you needing to find a bride would force it out of you, but I was starting to think we were playing chicken and you were actually going to make me have to bring it up." She pressed a hand to her chest. "God rest your grandfather's soul, he and I had a wager going. He was convinced you were going to wait until you were at the altar with a woman to admit it. My money was on you not letting it get that far." She pointed at the sky. "I told you so," she said to him before looking back at me.

My mouth was hanging open. "You've let me go through all this hell?" I was a little pissed.

"Well we weren't sure darling. I can't just insist my grandson is homosexual when he is made out to be the biggest womaniser in Britain by most of the tabloids."

"Okay, I have to give you that, but I was trying to keep it from you." I paused. "Wait, I thought you didn't read the papers."

"And I thought you liked women."

I slumped back in my chair. "I didn't knock up an American, but I am in love with one."

She sighed. "Now that is a real disappointment. A whole

country full of eligible men and you have to find an American?"

"You did send me to Canada."

"At least he's not Canadian, tossers."

"I wonder what they'd say if they heard you."

She grinned. "I'd claim I was senile."

I rolled my eyes. "Like anyone would believe that."

She sipped her tea, with a knowing look.

"I think I need to come out."

"I would agree with you."

"Do you think they'll disqualify me? I don't want Anne to be stuck in my shoes." Especially knowing she was gay too.

"Princes don't become kings. You were either born a king or not. It's in your blood, in your mannerisms and your poise. It can't be taught, and the people will respect you for it. You were meant to be the King. Parliament be damned. I approve this match with all my heart, and we'll make them change it."

My cheeks were damp. She was spectacular and right. I shouldn't have to hide what I am or who I love. No matter which gender that person is.

"All that matters to me is does he deserve you?"

"He doesn't know he does, and it's going to be hard to convince him to do this for me."

"He'll do it for you if he loves you. If he won't do it, no matter how much you love him, he's not the right person."

"He might need more time."

"You have some, but not much before there are rumours. It would be better to acknowledge than to dodge the papers."

"I know."

"Take some time and let me know. I stand with you

whatever you decide."

XAVIER

When I walked into my apartment, I felt like I needed a year to decompress and not talk to anyone. I left my phone on airplane mode after I got off the plane. It would be too easy to jump on the internet and find out every little thing Louis was doing. Stalk his every movement, and I was trying not to be that person, so it was safer to leave it off. He'd probably be announcing his engagement because he was hurt I left anyway. My mind loved to create worst case scenarios and run with them. It was kind of a specialty of mine.

I had a whole six hour flight of nothing but building up scenarios in my head while watching shitty movies. I'd also drawn him half a dozen times, which hadn't helped at all. I left my suitcase by the door of my loft and stripped down. I was going to spend the entire rest of the week in bed and maybe eat a tub of ice cream. I'd seen two movies on the flight that suggested it would help. So at some point I was going to have to get on the internet and order groceries because I was sure everything in my fridge was rotten at this point.

I'd just climbed under my thick down blanket when there was a knock on my door. I pulled a pillow over my head. It was probably my across the hall neighbor who was an eighty year old woman who acted like she was still in her mid thirties. She probably wanted to gossip and make sure I wasn't dead.

The knock on the door sounded again. "Not right now, Mrs. Hortenmyer," I screamed.

"I'm not going away," called a voice I didn't expect to hear again.

I was out of bed and pulling open the door before I had time to decide it was against my better judgement. I wanted to grab him and pull him inside, and at the same time I wanted to slam the door in his face. I'd spent the day in agony and here he was dredging it all back to the surface. I wasn't sure I had the energy to walk away again.

"You know it's kind of shitty that you got on a plane and got all the way home before I could talk to you."

"I had to or I would never have left." I lifted my shoulders giving him a what look. "I can't go back there with you. Please don't ask."

"I came out to my grandmother."

"You can't. What about Anne?" I wanted to reach out and touch him. Hug him. Give him comfort of some sort. I wished I'd stayed and been there for him.

"This isn't about Anne. This is about me."

"But she'll become heir. What will happen to her? You know she can't deal with it."

"Anne will be fine. She doesn't have to worry about being Queen. It won't come down to that."

"What? Then who?"

"Can we step inside?" He looked around. "I'd prefer not to have this conversation in the hall."

So he wasn't out-out then. I stepped back, allowing him into my tiny loft. He looked around as he shed his overcoat. He turned his back on me. There wasn't a closet except in my bedroom, so I draped the coat that probably cost more than my rent over the back of the sofa.

"I get that it's a big gesture that you came, but I really can't be your secret, even if key people know." And I couldn't. Just because the Queen knew and could find him someone suitable to be his 'wife' didn't make it okay.

I started to make some tea to clear my head.

"I'm going to come out publicly, I'm just going to choose the time and place carefully. It will be in an official announcement."

I dropped the coffee mug I'd been holding and didn't even react when it crashed onto the floor and exploded into a million pieces, sending scalding coffee and glass everywhere.

"Fuck." I bent to try and pick up the pieces noticing I'd splattered coffee all over Louis' pants. "I'm sorry. I'm sure I have something you can wear."

I got to my feet to go grab something to clean the mess, but he grabbed my arm, stopping me. "Leave it."

"I can't leave coffee all over both of us and the floor."

His grip tightened. "Listen to me."

I looked into his eyes and waited. "You were right. I need to do this for all the people who live in places they can't come out. For all the kids whose parents would kick them out. I'm coming out. I'm not abdicating. I've spent my entire life protecting Anne, and I don't plan to stop, but my grandmother said she will have my back on this. If Parliament has an issue with a gay king then they'll have her to deal with and a good portion of the country. Something like sixty percent support gay rights. Nothing like the trash fire that's going on over here." He gave me a smile at that.

My ears were ringing, and my hands were shaking. "Are you here to tell me you're marrying Drake or something before I find out?"

He blinked at me. "What?"

"It makes logical sense. He's the regal type." I forced a smile to my face. "I'm glad you decided to come out. It really is the best thing to show people." And I was happy for him and gay rights, but I was crushed for myself.

"You really think that's what I'm saying?" His fingers bit into my skin, and there was profound sadness in his eyes.

"How could it not be?"

"I'm not marrying anyone right now."

"Just going to let them get used to the idea." I nodded, wanting to fucking sink into a wall. I wanted to be alone. I wanted to throw things.

"I did plan on dating someone."

My eyes flashed back up to meet his. "Who?"

He laughed and looked at the ceiling. "You really are daft, aren't you?" He slid a finger under my chin and leaned in to brush his lips over mine. "I mean you."

Something in me broke. "No." Fear closed in on me as I saw my face on every single damn paper in the country.

"No?" There was still amusement dancing in his eyes. "What do you mean no?"

"How can you bring me out in public?" My fingers went to my face and my legs started to give out.

"Whatever do you mean?" There was so much confusion on his face.

"Look at me."

"I am looking at you." He laid his forehead against mine.

"Do you know what they'll say about me? This is my job. Let's see." I could see the bold headlines in my mind. "How about 'Most eligible bachelor in the world skips beauty and goes for the beast'."

He was trying not to laugh, I could see it on his face.

"What's so funny?"

"I always was rather attracted to the beast."

"This is not a time to make jokes." I ground my teeth. He just wouldn't understand, born with his perfect face.

"But it's funny."

"Funny that you're attracted to a monster?" I asked.

"I don't know what you see when you look in the mirror, but I know what I see when I look at you, and I've been attracted to you since I first saw you. I think you're lovely."

"You're the only one, and it's because you see past the scar."

He shook his head. "No, when I first saw you at the club I talked to you because of your looks, as shallow as that sounds. I've never been more attracted to someone in my life." He traced his thumb over the part of my scar above my lip.

"I don't think I can do it." The thought of people taking my picture. Chasing me down like I knew would happen with whomever the prince was with. It made my stomach turn.

His brows knit together, and he looked dejected. "Why

241

not?"

"Because I've been on this side of it. I'd be hounded twenty-four hours a day. No privacy. I'll never be alone again. And more than that I'm a nobody." Amidst the coffee and glass he pulled me closer just as my legs started to give out.

He kept me afloat and looked into my eyes. "It doesn't matter where you came from, or that you're 'nobody'. You're who I want. It's important enough to me to come out and face the world and let them know I'm gay. So I guess the question would be, do your feelings match mine?"

Well now I was pissed. "You're not the only one with feelings. It killed me to leave, and I almost didn't. If I'd gone one more day in there with the way you look at me when you wake up I wouldn't have been capable of walking away. I would have sacrificed it all just to get that tiny part of you. So don't tell me I don't have feelings."

A little smile started to turn on his lips. "So you'd be my secret, but when I'm offering the world and the crown, you throw it back at me?"

I groaned and pulled out of his grasp. "Because I'm not fit."

"Who gets to say you're fit?" He followed me to the kitchen as I grabbed towels to clean up the mess. He helped and we worked side by side in silence on our knees. "You told me I should come out and be gay in public and that it would do us a load of good."

"Yeah, but I didn't mean with me. I know I'm not fit to be your— Consort? Is that what they call it?"

"Do you have a fear of titles?" The way he rolled his eyes and shook his head with the little smirk told me who he was thinking. He thought I was crazy.

"Just because most people would kill for a title doesn't mean I would. I don't want fame. I only wanted you."

"Well the title comes with me. I can't do anything about it. You know why I can't. If I marry, my husband will be the Prince Consort. That won't change."

I wrinkled my nose and scoffed. "I really don't want to be a prince, ever."

"King Consort then," he said, giving me the cocky smile that made me want to do anything he asked.

"Are you even allowed to do that?" I was trying not to let his intoxicating joy cloud what the real problem was. I didn't think I could do this.

"I'll be King, I'm guessing I can do whatever I want to an extent." And he was still grinning. "For my husband, nothing would be too much."

"Stop talking to me about marriage," I snapped.

"Then talk to me about being my boyfriend."

I sat back on my heels and looked at him. "And what if it doesn't work out?" Or I can't do it. I added silently.

"Then it doesn't, but I think it's worth a chance."

I threw down the towel and scrubbed a hand over my face. "I think I need a shower." I got up, leaving the glass on the floor to be dealt with later.

"Okay…" he sighed and stayed where he was.

"Are you coming?" I asked.

The gleam was back in his look. "Is that a subtle yes?"

"Don't push it."

LOUIS

I wasn't going to ask any more questions. So I followed him. After the coffee incident I needed to shower anyway. With him it was a bonus. He could have sent me in there with a towel and told me to clean up. I started to unbutton my shirt as I entered the bathroom, but I paused as he started to undress. He was a sight. I didn't know what he saw when he looked in the mirror, but I saw perfection. There was a kindness in his eyes no other person I'd met bore, and no one who would want to marry me had. He didn't want to marry, which I thought was a good sign, not something I'd tell him but something I'd tell my grandmother to reassure her he wasn't after my title or money.

He looked up to find me looking. "You." He shook his head. "Don't read into this." He crossed the small distance between us and slipped his arms around me.

"A convenience shag?" I asked, knowing it was nothing of the sort.

He glared at me.

"So hostile. We should start experimenting with that in bed." I wiggled my brows.

He shoved me back into the basin and started to help me with my clothes. I finished my shirt and slid it off.

"I'm going to have to have Doug bring up my bag."

He pushed my slacks down my hips and then looked at me. "He's waiting in the car, isn't he?"

I shrugged.

"The man deserves a raise for as often as he has to wait on you while we fuck."

"I can't deny it." I stepped out of the ruined trousers, and he left to go turn on the water. Missing his touch already, I came up behind him as he bent over. I not so subtlety pressed my dick into his arse.

He glared over his shoulder but rocked his hips into my dick.

"So we're going with aggressive?" I asked.

His eyes were alight with lust, and I was liking my chances. I slid my dick along the split of his arse as he straightened, turning in my arms much too soon.

"Get in the damn shower."

I did as I was told, and when he didn't follow right away, I blanched and looked out of the curtain.

"Do I have you worried?" he asked.

"You did leave Britain and not answer your phone."

He threw a loofah at me. "I did that because—" He dropped his head, not making a move to join me. "Because I have feelings and I knew if I stayed I wouldn't ever be able to leave."

"You have feelings?" I repeated. I'd suspected but to hear him say it.

"What did you think this was?"

"I hoped."

He got in the shower but kept his distance. I stood under the spray waiting for him to join me. At last he did, pressing his body into mine.

"You're a little slow, you know?" he asked.

"Sure, I know. But why do you say so?"

"Do you really think I came to hide away with you in London for just a fuck?"

I lifted one shoulder. "It was a free trip to London. Others have used me for less."

"And you thought I was like them? We didn't leave the hotel the entire time we were there."

"No, I've never thought that about you."

He nodded and slid his hand down to my arse. "Does this mean I can fuck you without a condom?" he asked.

If his body hadn't already had me hard, that would have done me in.

"Have you been tested?" he asked.

"Three months ago, but if you want me to be again, I will."

"No, I trust you. I've always trusted you." And it was true. It was part of the reason I'd fallen for him. He was the most honest guy I'd ever met.

"I believe you." His lips brushed over mine, softly at first and then with the vigour I was expecting from the absence.

My lips parted with his, and my hands explored his wet body, and then something occurred to me. "Wait, don't you want to know when I was last tested?" I asked.

He smiled into my lips, skimming his fingers over my entrance, making it hard to concentrate.

"I'm sure you're tested all the time, and you did say it had been a while before me."

I narrowed my eyes at him and amusement showed in his look.

"What? You said it, not me." He slipped a hand between us, and all thought went out the window as he stroked both our cocks in unison.

I pumped my hips into his hand and drew in a ragged breath.

"You know there were quite a few hours I believed I'd never get this again," I said as I watched what he was doing.

"You're just with me because I'm good in bed, aren't you?"

I moaned as he squeezed over our tips. "It's at least seventy percent."

"Great way to pick a monarch." He was getting aggressive with his hand, and I could barely form words.

"As if every single queen before wasn't chosen in such a way. I doubt even my grandmother had better intentions. I've seen pictures of Charles. He was a looker back in the day."

Xavier grimaced. "I really don't want to hear about your hot grandfather."

"I'm the one who should be grossed out. Not you." I laughed and then dropped my face to his shoulder as he twisted his hand.

"Fair." He dropped to his knees, and I slumped back against the wall as he took me in hand. "And now I'm going to swallow your cock."

I moaned my response and then came down his throat.

GOTHA ÆTURNUM

LOUIS

Once we were dry, Doug brought up my things and we sat in sweats on Xavier's sofa. Neither one of us was speaking, and Doug had gone to get food once he decided I wasn't going to get shot inside his loft.

"How do we do all this? I mean if I decide to?"

"Well, we don't have to do it yet, but I will come out in due time, and then at some future date when you're comfortable we will put out a public statement through the House of Gotha, the royal family's official publication and say we are indeed seeing each other. Usually, things are only put out when there is an engagement, but this is a little different."

"Maybe we shouldn't." He looked a little dizzy.

"Shouldn't date?" There was disappointment written on my face.

"No, shouldn't put out a statement."

"You know as soon as we are seen in public you're going to be hounded. I mean I'm sure you know better than anyone else," I said carefully.

It took him a few tries before he got words out. "It was my job to do the hounding. We won't get any privacy."

"I know, and I completely understand if you back out at any point."

He put his head between his hands. "Whenever you say back out, I think of having to just be your friend, and you're coming out anyway so some other man would have you, touch you, go to bed with you. And you could become this whore you have the reputation of being." His lip lifted in disgust. "I'm not a jealous bastard, but I really don't like the idea of anyone else, or lots of others, having you. But the fact remains, if a statement isn't usually released until we—you're engaged, then don't treat it any differently."

"We can talk about what we want to do if you feel strongly about it." I paused, then it clicked what he said, and a smile started to pull at my lips. "You're not backing out?"

He turned to look at me, brushing his knuckles over my cheek. "I don't want anyone else to have you. As selfish and horrible as it sounds, and out loud it sounds even worse than in my head, it's true."

My smile got so wide my cheeks hurt.

"What?" he asked.

"You don't know how much I like hearing that."

"So we are doing this, but what now?" He looked a little like a lost puppy.

"I told you, the statement and all…"

He shook his head, cutting me off. "No, the dating. My job, the countries between us."

"Well, you are a photographer. There is other work you

could do, correct?"

He nodded, looking a little dejected.

"I'm sorry," I murmured.

"I get why I can't keep doing what I do. It's bad enough I did."

"Not terrible, but it's not something the royal household will want to focus on when they do profiles of you when the time comes—" I trailed off. He probably had no idea that I was as serious as I was, but that's how it worked in my position.

He looked green and like he was having a hard time breathing.

"And well…" I slipped a hand around the back of his neck. "I was hoping you'd move."

He looked up sharply. "Already?"

"Well, we are already doing this. We'd had time to get to know one another, and if we are going to give it a go I'd rather it be serious." I was putting a lot into this. Coming out for him. Long distance wasn't worth it for me.

"I am serious about you, Louis."

There was nothing he could have said to make me more happy. "So you'll come?"

"Want to stay here while I make arrangements?"

I nodded and chuckled.

"What?" he asked.

"Doug is going to love it."

That made him smile. "Will it be too inconvenient?"

He lifted his shoulders in a shrug. "It might be hard because you don't have a spare bedroom, but there might be another apartment in the building he can rent. How long do you think it will be."

"Well…" He scrubbed a hand down his face. "I have to tell all the people I used to work for. Most won't care. They only buy when I have pictures. As for Eran though. He's going to be sore." He scrunched up his face, and I couldn't blame him. What we'd done on Eran's dime wasn't great. "I need to look into renting this place and then pack. Look for a reputable job there."

I leaned over to reach inside my bag. "The job part will be easier than you think. I had Anne ask around, and she has a few leads for you."

He took the stack from me in awe. "When did she do this?"

"When I was stuck in the air for eight hours getting here."

He didn't unfold them. "You've really thought this all out, haven't you?"

"I have."

He pressed a hand into his chest. "Okay."

I slipped my hand into his. "Do you want this? Because I don't want you to feel like you have to for any reason."

He swallowed a few times. "You mean just because you're good in bed?"

"I've never thought you wanted me for any reason other than me and of course my glorious dick."

"Humble."

"Princes don't have to be."

"I do want this, I just wish your title didn't come with it," he admitted.

"Most days I feel the same."

He looked around his place. "When are we going back?"

"As soon as you're ready."

"That might be never."

"We have at least a little time. The Queen said she'd cover while I convinced you."

Or so I thought, until he turned on the TV and we saw the headline.

PRINCE LOUIS CONFIRMED GAY BY EX LOVER

XAVIER

We just stared at the television, neither one of us speaking. My phone started ringing off the hook. It buzzed, then rang, then buzzed so hard it nearly fell off the table. Message after message, emails, calls. People were scurrying for a story. I'd been on this story. Eran even offered to let me come on FMZ with a guest spot to talk about what I saw and if I suspected.

My heart hammered in my ears and halfway through reading my messages my chest stopped expanding. I couldn't draw in air. My mind felt like it was running on overdrive. It wouldn't stay focused, and breathing, breathing just wasn't happening. My ribcage was stuck in a vice grip by some invisible hand, and I was pretty sure this was it for me. I was going to die right here on my sofa before I got to even tell Louis how much he meant to me.

"Xavier?" Louis' voice barely got past the ringing in my ears.

I turned to look at him, but I'd used all the oxygen in my

lungs, so talking was out.

"You don't look so good."

I started to slip off the sofa as blackness ate around the corners of my vision. I was having a panic attack. It had been years. I'd been so careful. I knew my limits. I'd even been doing okay with this public stuff.

Louis was on his knees next to me shaking me. He was on the phone with someone. I really hoped he hadn't called 911.

"Xavier. Can you just tell me you're okay?" He was shaking me.

I tried to lift my arm to squeeze his shoulder, but it was so heavy. I put my head between my knees and focused on trying to breathe in and out. Pulling air into my lungs was a task, and I couldn't focus on Louis and do it. But I really didn't want to pass out.

Slowly but surely I got some oxygen, and my vision started to come back, but I kept my head down. If I sat up too fast I'd pass out. So I stayed hunched over. As my senses started to come back I felt his hand on me. He was rubbing my back and talking to me.

There was a loud bang and Doug was at my side. "Want me to carry him to the car?"

I was enough in control of myself again to get words out. "No." It wasn't forceful, but it was firm. "I'll be okay in a few minutes," I managed.

There was stone cold silence. A few more minutes passed, and I used the floor to help me get my head out of between my legs. I was stiff from staying in the position so long, but I managed to get off my knees and sit back against the sofa with Louis' help.

He and Doug kept exchanging words. The TV was off, which I was thankful for. I had no idea where my phone had gotten to but I didn't want to see it either.

"Want to get the door?" Louis asked Doug.

He nodded, backing away slowly but not leaving.

I avoided making eye contact with either of them. I closed my eyes.

"Are you okay?" Louis asked at length.

"I will be."

"Panic attack?" he asked.

I nodded still not looking at him. "And now you see more of why I'm unfit."

To his credit he didn't take his hands off me or back away. "It doesn't make you unfit."

I laughed. "Yes it does."

"Is it social anxiety?"

"I guess you can call it that. It's since all of this." I gestured at my face. "It got too hard to deal with everyone talking about it, and I guess I internalized too much of it for too long. I let it build up and by isolating myself more and more to not deal with it I did this." I shrugged. "Or so my therapist says."

"You see someone?"

"Yeah, not as often as I probably should. She helped. There were a few years where I wouldn't leave my house for weeks at a time."

"How'd you do that with your job?" he asked.

"I'd get a big payday and then live off it until I couldn't anymore. When I realized what I was doing to myself I started to see her. It's been better. I hadn't had a panic attack in years, but—" I finally looked at him. "But this is…it's a lot."

He nodded, and I was dying to know what he was thinking. If he was just waiting until I calmed down before he ran far away.

"Are you going to tell me how you got it?" He raised a hand to brush over my cheek, and I leaned into his touch craving it. I'd kill to understand what he saw in me.

"It's really not a great story."

"I'm sorry. I'll drop it if you don't want to talk about it. You're already doing so much coming with me." And there was the look. I knew the look in his eyes. It was the look of sorrow.

"Please don't look at me like that."

"Like what?" he asked

"Like what everyone else assumes. That I was beat by my dad or some shit. Or gay bashed, or I don't even know. But that sympathetic look. It's almost more painful than wearing the damn thing."

"I'm sorry, it wasn't what I was thinking at all."

"Then what were you thinking?"

"I was thinking, I wish you could see yourself through my eyes. Because to me you're exquisite, and there are no words that can do justice to the emotion I feel when looking at you." His words warmed me.

"I've spent most of my life being stared at, and I can assure you're the only one who finds me—" I shrugged, trying not to get emotional. "Whatever you think."

"I highly doubt as much. There is no way I'm the only one who sees you, but I'll be happy not to have any competition as I want to keep you to myself."

I half smiled. "You're a little insane."

"As long as you love me." He looked like a deer in the headlights after he said the words.

"I do." My smile broadened.

"You do?" The look in his eyes would kill me one of these days. If I could bottle that look I may just start feeling better about myself.

I nodded holding his gaze.

"I love you too," he said in a whisper like if he uttered it too loud it would shatter the moment.

I looked down, still grinning. "I'll tell you if you really want to know."

He stepped closer so our bodies were flush. "Please."

"It's stupid. So stupid, and it changed my entire damn life." It was so damn painful to talk about. To think about.

"You can tell me," he urged.

"I was running around my house. Like all kids do I'm sure, and my parents had this glass coffee table. I loved to play on it. I'd stand on it and jump off of it. It freaked my mother out. She constantly told me not to get on it, that I was going to fall through it. She was constantly hovering, but every time she turned her back I was somewhere else lost in my imagination and back on the table. She begged my father to buy a new table, and he told her they couldn't afford it. It was pretty and from a time before they'd had kids." I pressed his face in to my shoulder lost in the memory.

"I fell through it. I can still feel it. The glass. The scars on my hands are gone, and well my legs were mostly unharmed, but one of the large pieces caught me as I was coming down, and it was bad. So bad." I shook my head like I could change the past with a wish. "There was so much blood. Our living room carpet looked like someone had been murdered. My mom called 911 as she held me in her arms. I was thrashing and screaming and she was trying to get the bleeding to stop." My voice hitched, and it was hard to go on.

He didn't press. He let me have a moment.

"I don't remember the rest. Or the stitches. I was in the hospital for a couple of days. My parents, well my dad was a blue collar factory worker, they couldn't afford a plastic surgeon, so it was the best the ER doctor could do...but it changed everything."

"It was an accident. It may have changed things, but it made you who you are, and I love who you are."

"Fuck how I look, I hate it, but...that's not it. Every time I look at myself and see it I have to know I ruined their marriage. I couldn't listen. It was my fault. I did this to myself, but they didn't deserve this. My father didn't deserve it. My mother never looked at him the same. She was so angry." I took a shaky breath. "And he never got over her. He died alone and still in love with her."

There was so much emotion there in every look. He had the most expressive face I'd ever seen, and he saved me in those moments with all the love in his eyes.

"It wasn't your fault. You were a kid. Kids make mistakes, and you can't hold all the blame for that the rest of your life."

"Part of me knows that. And when we go see him, my dad, and she leaves flowers on his grave, part of me thinks that maybe they just needed something to bring them back together but ran out of time."

He stroked hand down my back. "You deserve to be happy and can't blame yourself for issues in their marriage. It was an accident."

"If you realize how right I was about not being able to do this and want to leave, you can."

His brow creased in the center and then he looked pissed. "Are you kidding me?"

I shook my head. "I wouldn't blame you."

"I'm asking for more than any person on the planet could possibly ask you for. I'm not going to run away at the first sign of trouble."

"But how can we do this?"

"The news cycle is going to be about me being gay for awhile. There was nothing about me dating anyone. They don't even know where I am. I haven't been photographed in two weeks, and we can keep us on the down low as long as you need. You can move into Kensington with me, and we can stay in." He slid a hand around the back of my neck and pressed his forehead to mine. "I'm sure they'll figure it out eventually, but we can minimize it at long as possible."

"Okay." I wasn't sure what else to say.

"Are you sure? Because you are allowed to back out."

"You're worth going through this." My words made him smile, and that was enough for now.

I got some food in me and was feeling almost human again a few hours later. We'd returned to our sedentary lifestyle in my place. We played video games, and binge watched TV. Doug had gotten an apartment in the building, and as long as we promised not to leave, he left us alone for the most part. Probably because I was in a loft and he didn't want to hear or see us fucking and we were still fucking like rabbits.

My mind started to function again late into the night. We'd

stuck to streaming so neither of us had seen the news, and after a quick call with his grandmother he'd pretended nothing was going on, but now questions started to filter into my brain.

"Louis?"

He looked over. "Yes?"

"If you've had all one night stands and no relationships, how is this coming from a former lover?"

He sighed. "I've been thinking about that a lot, and I'm not sure you want the answer."

"I don't like the sound of that. Is there something you haven't told me?" I could tell just by watching his face there was. "Tell me."

"I saw Drake that day I was coming back from the palace. He saw me in the street before I went inside. I didn't think much of it..." he trailed off.

"You think he would have done this."

He looked out the window. "I don't know. I've been going over it in my head all day. Who else could it be? Few people know, and they've all signed NDAs." He shook his head and looked at his hands. "They could have risked it and left their name out of it, or maybe it's Drake because I turned him down and he figured out why."

"I'd hate to think that of him." Really I believed it, but it would suck for Louis if his old friend was that spiteful. "To force you out of the closet? He should know better since he's one of us."

"I know, and I don't want to ask him."

Louis's phone started to ring and he frowned at it, checking his watch. "I guess it's morning there." He pressed to answer it and mouthed at me. "It's Anne."

His expression grew dark as he listened. He pulled away from me and leaned forward to rest his elbows on his knees.

When he looked at me I knew it was bad. "Maybe you should turn the television back on."

I flipped it off the steaming service and on to Star News. And there was my apartment on display. My head started to spin, and I imagined my face on the cover of every paper, and my stomach started to do back flips. I managed to keep myself breathing but just barely.

We watched in silence for a few minutes. There was all kinds of speculation on who the prince was held up with. They had my name. Thankfully there were no pictures of me...yet.

"Xavier." His hand was on my back. "I'm so sorry."

I leaned into him, trying to take solace in him.

"How?"

"Anne confirmed Drake figured it out. He saw you leave the airport with Doug and then he followed you two and waited to see if I'd come. It took him a while to figure out who you were. But the longer we were held up in the hotel the more he seethed I guess. Then he saw Anne and he asked about you. In passing. She'd thought I'd told him." Louis looked entirely distraught. "He asked about me and then about my guy, and all Anne said was 'Oh you know about Xavier? He's great for Louis, isn't he?' and well with your first name he put the rest together."

"But how did he get my damn last name?" I was more angry at the moment than panicked. I knew that douche was bad news.

Louis looked at me with a profound sadness in his eyes. "The hotel was in your name. He charmed it out of the staff once he knew your first name. He pretended like he'd forgotten and yeah, if you act like you need information and have a little bit..."

We went back to watching in silence.

"We can't stay here now."

"No," I agreed.

"If you want me to go..." He closed his eyes, awash with emotion.

LOUIS

The pain I felt radiating from him was too much to bear. I slipped my arms back around him and brushed my lips over his. "Truly, if I leave now, you can stay inside for a few weeks and they'll get bored. I never meant to bring this all down on you."

"Let's leave tonight."

I stared at him. "Excuse me?"

"Let's go. I'll hire someone to rent the place." He shrugged looking around his loft. "I'll get a flat there and we'll stick to the plan. I'll minimize going out, until the story is old. I have savings I can live on until I get a job."

He was working through all of this in his head. I could see the fear in his eyes, but there was resolution there too.

"You're sure?"

He cupped the side of my face. "What other choice do I have?"

"You have choices." I hated that he felt like they'd been

taken from him. Because of me.

"Not if I want this to work, and that's okay."

"You know you sound more reasonable than I do at the moment."

He gave me a half smile.

We were out of his place before the sun came up the next morning. He had most everything he owned packed into a few boxes Doug had picked up and two suitcases. And here we stood in the hall outside his door as he leaned back against the wall breathing hard. The boxes and bags were loaded in the car, and now it was just a matter of getting Xavier in the car.

The paparazzi smelled blood since they saw Doug loading the stuff. They weren't leaving for anything. I'd even offered to leave before Xavier and have him follow in a few days, but Doug figured it would be dangerous, and Xavier, knowing how their minds worked, knew they'd camp there until he showed his face.

"Are you okay?"

He gave me a flat look.

"I don't know what else to say," I admitted.

"I think I need to do this on my own terms."

I frowned at him. "Walk out there by yourself? Not a chance."

He shook his head. "Come back inside for a few."

Confused as fuck I followed him back inside where he promptly climbed back in bed. Fuck.

"Xavier?" I asked getting worried.

"Come here."

"I know we don't have a plane to catch, but going back to

bed?" I took a tentative step towards him.

"Have a little faith."

I crossed the room and sat on the edge of the bed. "What's going on? If you can't do this, we really don't have to leave..." I didn't know what else to say.

"Lay down with me." He had his phone out and was turning it back on.

"Going to check your messages?" I slid in with him, shoes and all.

He opened his camera and pulled me in close, so both our faces fit in the photo and it started to dawn on me what he was doing.

"Eran?" I asked.

"Yeah."

He took a few photos changing the angle of his face as he did. Trying to minimize the look of his scar I guessed. He grunted and stopped.

"Good enough I guess." He sat up and looked over at me.

"Are you okay with me sending in this photo? You can always deny it of course. Hell, we can claim my phone was hacked."

I put my fingers on his lips to silence him. "It will be fine. If this is the way you want to do it."

"Well, I was thinking. I did this on his dime. I know I did my job, but it wasn't honest. The least I can do is do it this way. My face will already be out there, that way all those photos out there won't matter as much, and maybe I'll care a little less once it's all over."

I sat up and pressed my lips to his. He smiled into my lips and brought the phone to his ear.

"Eran?"

He listened.

"Yeah, I know. I can't say anything. I did my job, and well we started talking. It wasn't intentional."

He sat back.

"I'm not going to give you an exclusive. We aren't going to talk about it right now."

He was listening again, and I was starting to get frustrated with only hearing one side of the conversation. Xavier must have been able to read my face because he put it on speaker phone and held it between us.

"X, it's the least you could do. Throw me a bone. Give me a statement. Something to go on. I feel like a douche trying to run a photo of my own fucking guy. I don't even have a damn employee photo of you because you're a fucking contractor. I feel so behind in this. No one has it. How the hell do you not even have a Facebook? I've never met someone I know more off the grid."

"Eran."

He stopped his ramble. "What?"

"I'm going to send you an exclusive, but you didn't get it from me. If pressed, say it's privileged. No one is going to come after you for it. I might talk big, but I swear to you as long as you keep it quiet that it didn't come from me you won't have any issues. I don't have time for anything, I don't want anything from you, just your word."

"What is it?"

"A picture you're going to want to print immediately. I'll give you an hour lead on it." Xavier looked at me and I nodded.

He mouthed sex and winked. I grinned. I was sure we

could give him an hour.

"A picture of what?" Eran asked.

"I'm emailing it to you now." Xavier waited for him to open it.

"HOLY SHIT."

"I thought so."

"This might make up for you not telling me you were fucking the prince on the side."

"I never said I was."

He scoffed.

"For all you know nothing started until I was off your dime."

"Sure buddy," Eran muttered.

"We're even. I'm quitting and not working anymore."

"No fucking shit." Eran laughed. "But we aren't even." I could tell he was joking the way he said it, and Xavier ignored it.

"So you're printing it?"

"It's been on the air since I opened it."

I could tell Xavier was starting to have issues breathing. "Remember what I said," he said, with half a stutter.

"I got you. We didn't speak."

"Thank you," I said.

"Louis? Holy shit. There was speculation you were there with him."

"Just have your guy here ready to take photos in an hour. As a personal thank you from me."

Xavier hung up the phone, and I jumped him before he could focus too much on what was now out there.

LOUIS

Xavier: Where are you?

Louis: Inside, why?

Xavier: Because now that I've been paraded around London and half the countryside in a carriage like a show pony, I'm coming to get my revenge.

Louis: You can't see me before the wedding.

Xavier: What are you, the blushing bride?

Louis: You're the one who got paraded around London. Just saying.

I couldn't help but laugh. I felt bad for him. I really did.

Xavier: When I find out who got me the damn carriage instead of the Rolls Royce, heads will roll. I'm bringing the guillotine back.

Louis: You can't kill the Queen.

I could just imagine him standing there with narrowed eyes, not sure if he should trust it was her. It was clearly me, but since he'd gotten used to his face being on every paper in the world, I wanted photos of it. And they were so hard to get in a car. All the gay kids around the world needed to see him about to marry a prince.

Xavier: Tell me where you are.

Louis: In the confessional.

Xavier: This isn't a Catholic church.

Louis: Well damn, that sounded kinky.

The door opened and in walked Xavier, his cheeks a little flushed from the fresh air. He had a look in his eyes and I knew I was in for it.

"It's bad luck to see me," I pressed.

"At least you're admitting you're the bride before I fuck you."

"We're in a church."

"We're in Windsor Castle. We aren't in the church yet," he replied already starting on my trousers.

"Close enough."

"Are you objecting, your highness?"

I shook my head. "Not now, and not ever."

"Good. I'd hate to get all the way down the aisle in this get up only to have you object." He shoved down my pants and boxer briefs and grabbed my ass, hauling me to him.

"We are going to look like a wrinkled mess."

"Doug knows how to iron right?" He laughed and stepped back. "Go ahead. I know you're dying to fold them over the back of a chair."

I did just that, taking my time to remove the rest of my clothes. He was undressed from his monkey suit in half the time it took me and standing there with his hands on his hips as he watched me.

"We don't want to look like we just fucked in all our pictures."

"Why not?" he asked stalking towards me.

"Because this moment is going down in history. Do you want your post sex look to be the one immortalised for all time as the final breakthrough in equality? Besides, I'd like to be able to show our children some of them," I said as he pressed his body into mine.

That gave him pause. He looked into my eyes, and I couldn't tell if I'd scared him.

"Too soon?" I asked, knowing we'd been on a whirlwind of courting, coming out, him moving here, and now a wedding, all in the last eighteen months.

"No." A look came over his face I couldn't read. "I hadn't thought about it." There was another long pause before he went on. "I want that with you. Even if they have to be yours, I'm assuming."

"Not all of them have to be mine. Just the first." I hated saying it out loud, but that was one thing that would never fly.

"As long as we use the same donor for all of them, so they are related."

"They will be, and we're pretty sure there are royal heirs throughout history that didn't belong to their fathers, so really how mad could they be?"

He laughed and tilted his head, going for my neck. I moaned and went willingly as he started walking me back towards the sofa. It was white, and at least one hundred and fifty years old, but if I couldn't fuck on every piece of antique furniture, what good was being the future king? He shoved me back onto it but didn't join me. I gave him a questioning look.

"Bend over the back," he ordered.

Since doggy was a favorite of mine, I did as I was told, but instead of taking me, he dropped to his knees. I looked over my shoulder and whimpered.

"I've been wanting to do this awhile." His voice was low and sultry.

It went through me, sending electricity up my spine before his tongue even touched me.

"I wasn't sure you were into it."

"I have been in theory. Never tried it before."

His tongue stroked from my balls up my split, and my head dropped forward. I was going to have a hard time replying.

"Well—" I gasped. "You seem like a pro to me, and I'm going to be repaying the favour."

"Only if you want to."

"I insist," I said in more of a moan than words as his tongue worked over me. "If you keep that up I'm going to come before you even fuck me."

He licked and pressed his tongue into me, spreading me and opening me up. Out came a packet of lube as he got to his feet.

"I don't know how you carry those. If I did that it would burst and be all over my trousers."

"And be all over the papers." He slipped two fingers inside me, quickly distracting me from thought.

His head replaced his fingers, and he didn't take his time, forcing me wide open. He took what he wanted, aggressively, and I wouldn't have it any other way.

"Fuck your hand," he demanded.

"You just like ordering the prince around, don't you?"

"Damn right."

I took myself in hand and quickly brought myself to the edge, and we both let go, since we did have some place to be.

We'd laid on the sofa, wrapped around each other, putting it off for a few more minutes. His fingers stroked through my hair, and I didn't want to move, even if I was desperate to tie this man to me forever.

"You know I wouldn't change things for anything?"

"What do you mean?" I asked.

"I miss the privacy, but you are worth all of this."

I looked up at him and brushed our lips together. "I didn't think I'd ever be this happy."

He cupped the side of my face. "Nor I."

ACKNOWLEDGEMENTS

Kerry - I feel like everyone of these I write isn't enough. From beta reading, to British speak, to plot, cover, and formatting you are my rock and I couldn't do any of this without you.

Karen - For your amazing help in editing.

Sally - Love the comments, and even when you don't leave comments because you're too into it.

Lili - Thank you for all the help.

Jen - For all the Lobster things.

Virginia - For finding all my errors.

Judith - For all the advice and help getting this book out there.

Patty - And YOU because you said I left you out of the last.

Printed in Great Britain
by Amazon

54669728R00166